Deadly Nightshed

Deadly Nightshed

WILLIAM MANER

PUBLISHED FOR THE CRIME CLUB BY

DOUBLEDAY & COMPANY, INC.

GARDEN CITY, NEW YORK

1986

Anyone who believes that Pan is real will believe
that the characters and situations in this book are,
too. But the rest can be assured that they are
inventions of the imagination and do not represent
actual persons, living or dead.

Library of Congress Cataloging in Publication Data

Maner, William.
Deadly nightshed.

I. Title.
PS3563.A465D4   1986   813'.54   85-12938
ISBN 0-385-23259-4

First Edition

Deadly Nightshed

CHAPTER 1

Charles A. P. Cumberley, inevitably called Cap, stood at the window of his office overlooking the courthouse lawn and watched his secretary's daughter, Peaches, walk toward his building, pausing in the shade of the new-leafed maples to say something to the young sheriff's deputy Angus Bealle.

Barely seventeen, honey-haired, lush and ripe as her name, she wore a pink T-shirt and red running shorts one size too small. On one hip was a tiny cassette player. Its earpiece looped her neck, a precious collar. Whatever music entered her head, the siren call of Venus was what her pouting, pliant lushness transmitted. Her face had not yet lost its childish puffiness, but her eyes had no innocence. Peaches was her name, peaches her look. She had a ripeness that made the boys on the school bus go hard as hickory. It worried her father and tormented the principal, the coach, and the physics teacher at her high school.

At Buck Bolton's Exxon station across from the courthouse Bobby Horewood whistled loudly as he pumped gasoline into Kenyon Lynes's Volvo station wagon and watched Peaches walk across the street, then turned and looked boldly and frankly at Kenyon Lynes. The tune he whistled had a languorous, plaintive note. Kenyon Lynes turned reluctantly away from his youthful animalism as a car drove up to the pumps and a man waved to her. "Bitsy," she called. "We weren't expecting you until later." They exchanged a social kiss. Bobby Horewood continued whistling as he finished with Kenyon's Volvo and began filling the Buick belonging to the man she called Bitsy. He watched her drive off, then turned his attention to what his customer was saying. He never stopped whistling while he listened.

This sunny Friday in May belonged to the earthy spirit of the god Pan, and around the courthouse square in Phoebeville if you tuned in carefully you might pick up the woodsy god's pipes. Nobody in Bushanna County admitted hearing the pipes; there weren't three dozen Bushannans who would know what you were talking about. If they also knew those sudden frights that panic the soul, they put them down to dyspepsia. But what made the purebred bulls behind the white fences bellow and the cocks in the yards crow louder and the high school boys going home in the buses keep their hands in their pockets when they sat beside their sweet-smelling, giggling classmates? What made birds sing at midday and bedsprings creak at midnight?

Bushanna is a pleasant Virginia county, its rolling hills climbing to the Blue Ridge Mountains at its western border. Its lack of a railroad has kept it rural, which attracts a class of "come-heres" who build estates along the ridges, white fences around the hills, and curiosity among the natives. The natives get their mail at post offices called Phoebeville, Gabble's Grave, Petite Grange (pronounced Pee-tight), Adam's Union, Devil's Marker, Hullet's Tavern, Mount Tabor. The come-heres have their mail addressed to places called Copperfields, Castle Hill, View Halloo Farm, The Vixen's Den, Ardleigh.

The county had been formed in the reign of George III from portions of adjoining counties. Zeal for Good Queen Anne had loaded Virginia with rivers bearing her name: North Anna, South Anna, Rivanna, Rapid Anne, and the mighty James above the falls the Fleuve Anne. The Up Anna which flowed through Bushanna County had its headwaters in a mountain gap called Mouth of Anna. Latinizing and corruption had made it and the county Bushanna.

Cap Cumberley watched Peaches tantalize Angus with a laugh and a twist as she headed toward his office, and turned away when he caught his secretary watching him. If anybody in Bushanna County had tuned Pan's pipes out, it was Selma.

Peaches pushed the door open and stood almost waiting for applause at her entrance.

"Hi, Mom. Hi, Mr. Cumberley."

"What are you doing in town? I thought you were helping Mrs. Lynes this afternoon."

"I am, Mom. I drove in to town with her."

"Dressed like that?"

"What's the matter with the way I'm dressed?"

"I've told you before—"

Cap Cumberley picked up the mail and went into his office. He flipped through the letters Selma had handed him and slit open the envelope marked personal she had not opened. Selma Rillbon had seen him glancing at the tight seams of Peaches's shorts, at the nipples under the braless T-shirt. "My God, man, she's only seventeen!" he thought. "Men have been prosecuted for less."

Through the window he watched Kenyon Lynes make her way toward the Super-Buy Supermarket. Her bare shoulders, only partly shaded by her wide hat, caught the afternoon sunlight. She was tanned and trim, though it was only mid-May. Cap knew that she and Jack Lynes had taken their boat to the Caribbean and were now at Copperfields. It had been more than a year since he had seen her, how many years since he had taken her to bed? She was plumper now, but who wasn't? He imagined under her light dress her full breasts with the pink corona around the rising paps, not brown ones like Amy's. He hated brown ones.

He saw Peaches cross the lawn to wait for Kenyon at her car and saw them drive off. He knew this must be the weekend of Jack Lynes's Cock and Balls Club. Jack's randy uncle Fess Lynes, who had built Copperfields seventy years before, had named those golfing and cockfighting weekends he had hosted and Jack had kept them up when he inherited Copperfields. Five years ago Cap and Amy had been a part of them; Amy was probably at Copperfields today. Every spring and fall on a Friday night there'd be a cockfight in Jack Lynes's barn, and on Saturday they'd play golf all day and there would be a large party at night. He and Amy had been regulars before the fights, before the drinking, before the divorce, before he came running home to Phoebeville, before Emily's death.

Cap had quit wondering if Jack Lynes knew about Kenyon and him when he found out that Jack and Amy were meeting regularly on Jack's boat. That was after he found out about Amy and Fossy Glove—or was it before—after he had learned about Amy and his law partner Paul McFerlin? Cap turned from the window and pulled the letter from the envelope.

By ordinary human standards Sheriff Rowe's Pan-receiver should have been off that Friday afternoon. He was returning from a rendezvous with Mavis Stonebrunner who lived over near Petite Grange. Her husband, Clyde, a long-distance truck driver, was in Arkansas. Sheriff Rupert Rowe could not escape being called "Shad" any more than Wyndell Rhodes, the Bushanna agricultural agent, could miss being called "Dusty." Rowe was a big redheaded man whose earnestness concealed his slowness to grasp essentials. He looked taller than he was because he carried his shoulders high and saw that his uniforms were always sharply pressed. His imagination seldom rose above his belt, which had expanded gradually as the sheriff grew in years and experience. His attraction for women was hard to explain, except that his primary ambition was to bed every woman in Bushanna County before he had to quit.

Unlike the sheriff's office, which had been built in the 1930s with WPA money, the building that housed the commonwealth's attorney had stood on the courthouse lawn for two hundred years. Like the Bushanna County Courthouse, its soft red brick had mellowed over the centuries and its white-columned portico echoed the influence of Thomas Jefferson's architectural interest. It was widely thought but never proven that Jefferson had sketched the design for the courthouse and the dependencies surrounding it on the small square.

The wide wooden door had to be pushed hard; it sagged and jammed on the worn slate floor.

Sheriff Rowe walked into the commonwealth's attorney's outer office with a handful of papers. He waved them at Cap Cumberley as the lawyer came out of his office.

"Gonna see you at the Lynes's barn tonight?"

Cumberley shook his head. "Seems to me, Sheriff, you ought to be more discreet about that. After all, you're a police officer."

"Hell, Cap, you know as well's I do, it ain't against the law. The cockfighting I mean. It's just the gambling, if there is any, and the prizes, and that ain't nothing but a class-three misdemeanor."

"There wouldn't be any fights if there weren't gambling."

"All these years I never made no issue of it. There's prize money for the winners, but I ain't getting no warrants."

Selma Rillbon, Cumberley's secretary, quit her typing. "It's a mean, cruel business. I've never liked it."

" 'Scuse me, Selma, but roosters is born to fight. It's their nature, just like it's some men's natures. You can't keep them from fighting."

"You don't have to encourage it."

"You have to go with nature, Selma."

She turned away. "It's not my nature."

The sheriff followed Cumberley into his office. "Like it's man's nature to want a little hump now and again, you know what I mean." Cumberley had learned not to respond to such comments. "Don't you worry, Cap, there ain't going to be no trouble. Never has been. I'll see to that."

"What about those cockfights, Shad? Does Jack Lynes still have gamecocks at Copperfields, or are they brought in from other places?"

"Pat Rillbon keeps a few here and there for Lynes. But it's not like it used to be. Old Mr. Fess Lynes would raise straight up if he knew his nephew had let Copperfields' cockfights dwindle off to a few hack fights like this."

"I'd as soon see them quit altogether, to tell the truth. I'm surprised Jack Lynes keeps them up."

"Tradition, I suppose. Don't like to see things change. Around here, people expect things to be the same."

"My guess is he just doesn't have the guts to change things."

"There's nothing wrong with cockfights, Cap. Betting and prizes, that's just sport. Besides, we never enforced that law around here. People wouldn't stand for it. Did you know the gamecock almost got to be the national bird instead of the eagle? Lost out by one vote."

"How do you know that, Shad?"

"Read it somewhere. I remember when Mr. Fess Lynes was alive, they had real cockfights out there. Not just these hack fights. You go over to Charlottesville, down to Martinsville and Danville, go anywhere. They have good fights. Go on for two days."

"I'd be happier if Jack Lynes would cut them out entirely."

"He can't do that, Cap. His Uncle Fess started his golfing and cockfighting club sixty years ago. Cockfightin's a Virginia tradition."

"Yes. I know about those golf and cockfighting weekends." Cumberley dismissed the subject by picking up some papers. They spent half an hour on details of trials coming up the next week, and the sheriff stopped at Selma's desk on his way out.

"Your husband know how you feel about cockfighting, Selma?"

"It's a dirty business; I've told him so. He only does it because he works for Jack Lynes. You know that."

"They got a house full of folks up there, ain't they?"

"They're Mrs. Lynes's friends. They've been there for more than a week now, all of them dieting and exercising and having what they call intellectual discussions." Selma sniffed. Her thin taut figure wasn't soft like those women's, her sniff said. "Jeff says they're driving him crazy, always wanting to play tennis with him, or worse. He's got all he can do with his regular duties and his college classes. Peaches calls it Fat City."

The sheriff was smiling as he went out. He had his own ideas of how the rich and idle acted. If he was twenty-two, like Jeff Rillbon, in the middle of all that—Jesus!

CHAPTER 2

The barn was filled except for some seats in the front rows. There were forty or so men, a dozen women. Years before the seats from an old theater in Richmond had been installed in tiers around the cockpit by Fessenden Lynes. At the far end from the entrance a small door led to a room where the handlers kept their birds in cages until they were ready to fight. A cool breeze blew through the doors, but the air was strong with whiskey, tobacco, human bodies, and the sour scent of poultry.

The sheriff, out of uniform, had watched Jack Lynes come in with his guests as the fights started. He did not know their names, though he had seen them with Lynes at previous cockfights. Earlier he had checked the crowd, saw Jack Klaud, the state senator, with two men he did not know. Across the pit was Giff Heddick, the druggist from Phoebeville. In the upper seats he saw Randy Solverson, the owner of View Halloo Farm, with two boys from the local high school. The sheriff knew most of the people in the room and recognized some faces that were not known to him by name.

Kenyon Lynes waved graciously to the benches as she steered her guests to their seats. The fight in the pit had just started and the handlers courteously held it up until the Lyneses and their guests were seated. The fight was between a white and a dark gray, but when the referee called "Handle!" it was over before anyone could bet much money on it. In less than two minutes the gray had driven its gaff in a fury of feathers through the heart of its opponent. The owner of the white cut its steel gaffs from its legs, replacing them in the leather hip holster after wiping the blood off on his trousers and tossing the dead bird in a corner outside the ring. The victor took his bird away, smiling broadly at the cheers from the crowd.

There was a surge of interest among Jack Lynes's party when

the next fight began. Bobby Horewood was handling one of Lynes's fighters, pitted against a bird from Fluvanna County.

Bobby Horewood was twenty years old, thin and muscular, with a healthy animal quality he did not try to hide. He wore a denim shirt with the sleeves cut off, the buttons open to his waist. His jeans hugged his thin hips and thighs, leaving little question of the power under the bloodstained cloth. His mouth was full and wide, with a permanent half smile through which he piped his constant whistling melody, his nose straight and thin, with wide flaring nostrils. His dark eyes ranged openly through the stands whenever there was a break in the fighting, flashing at anyone who caught his attention.

The fight started furiously, Bobby's gray tearing into the red and the red fighting back, throwing its steel spurs with vicious skill, until both birds were bloody messes.

Bobby Horewood's jeans were covered with blood; he wiped his hands on his thighs and took a deep breath, blowing air down his bird's blood-congested lungs.

"Hey, man, he's going fast!" a voice yelled. Another called back, "He'll get him, you just watch!"

The referee under the bright fluorescent lights called "Pit!" and Bobby Horewood put his gray bird on the line. "Go on now. There he is!" he urged. The gray cock, bleeding from one eye, turned his good side toward the pit, looking for his enemy. Feathers flared. The two birds leaped, jabbed, hunted for an eye, a wattle. Somebody yelled "Shoot 'em!" as the red cock leaped, driving the long steel upward-curving spur into the gray.

The referee called "Handle!" and the men took up their birds, Bobby pulling the steel from the bleeding breast. The red had lost an eye. Its handler, a short dumpy man in his forties with a slight limp, put a finger down its throat and stretched its neck, trying to bring it back.

The red, hit again, went down. The referee called time, the handlers picked up their fighters and after a short conference with the referee took them to a pit smaller than the arena where they had been fighting, beyond the tiers of seats. There they fought until the red, falling over, had its head torn open by Bobby's victorious gray. A half dozen of the spectators left their seats to watch while another fight began in the main ring. Biston Barrell, the man Bobby had heard called Bitsy, joined them, congratulating Bobby and following him as he carried his bedraggled victor off, making small talk and watching as Bobby severed the head of the dying bird with a thin knife from a holster in his belt and tossed its body in a corner.

The next fight was under way when six people, four men and two women, came in. All of them wore bright sports clothes. The sheriff knew four of them. One of the women had a cockfighting barn at her place over beyond Charlottesville; the man in the red jacket was Mark Nailles; he'd seen him at cockfights in the area. A big sport, everybody said, but he could be mean. They waved and smiled at Jack and his party, and the handlers stepped back and held their birds while the newcomers settled down. The birds, aware of each other, jerked their legs and strained their necks. The gray with black wing and tail feathers had a flash of white across its saddle. The dark red shown like copper in the harsh light.

Mark Nailles, the man in the red jacket, said "Twenty-five on the red," and the senator held up his hand; another said, "Fifty on the gray," and Jack Lynes made a sign. In the upper rows the betting was quieter.

Released, the birds darted forward, then froze. The gray struck; in a rush of wings they rose two feet in the air. Both birds instinctively attacked from above and as instinctively tried to prevent the other from doing so. The red dropped first and the gray, taller though weighing the same, reached with its beak. A man called out "Eight to ten on the red," and one of Kenyon Lynes's guests, a tall dark-haired woman in gray slacks, raised her hand without looking around.

The birds were evenly matched. What the red lacked in height it made up in fight. It threw spurs fast. In less than a minute it had damaged the gray.

"Oh my God!" the small blond woman in a red dress, sitting with Kenyon Lynes said. "His eye! He's blinded in one eye!" The cocks lay at the edge of the pit, gasping. The handlers separated them and took them to the line. The handler of the gray licked the bird's bloody head and eyes until his mouth and face were covered with blood.

"He'll lick him with one eye," a man in the front row yelled when Sheriff Rowe called out "Ten on the red." The red took a gaff in the eye, evening the chances. They were pitted, fought, were pitted. The rattle of the birds' throats as they gasped for breath could be heard over the cheering. The gray staggered but held on. It caught the red in the other eye. "He'll lick you sightless," Rowe yelled.

"Fifty," Mark Nailles yelled, holding up his hand.

"Gotcha," the man beside Jack Lynes said as the handlers blew down the throats and licked the blood from their charges and waited for the referee at the line.

The woman in red stood up and cried out. "He's blind! For God's sake, Jack, stop this!"

In the silence that followed, the voice of Mark Nailles carried through the barn. "Oh shut up, you silly cow."

The woman ran around the pit and out of the barn. Kenyon followed her. "I don't care if he is my brother," Sheriff Rowe heard her sob. "He's no right—"

"Come on, fight," Nailles called to the referee. Two of the women in Jack Lynes's party after a moment rose and followed Kenyon. Only the tall dark-haired one remained. Bitsy Barrell, who had taken a seat beside her, looked up and watched his wife leave, then turned back to the fight.

The red staggered gamely, trying to find its rival by sound. In one wild fury it attacked, drove the gray to the edge of the pit in front of Lynes. The two gamecocks leaped into the air and the red flashed its wings in one last desperation before it fell dead at Biston Barrell's feet. He recoiled as blood from the ravaged fowl spattered his shoes and trousers. The woman in gray slacks reached down, picked up the thrashing body and threw it back into the pit, ignoring the blood that spilled on her.

The handlers picked up their birds and left the pit. The red's handler tossed the dead bird in a corner; the other took his winner outside and wrung his bleeding neck.

Halfway through the next fight Peaches appeared at a corner of the row of seats opposite Jack Lynes. The Hatch claret and the red were evenly matched; the fight had gone on for ten minutes. Peaches watched, her mouth half-open, her pink tongue showing, as Bobby Horewood blew air down his cock's throat. Jack Lynes saw the man in the red jacket watching her, his throat contracting as he swallowed hard.

Pat Rillbon moved around behind the seats to the corner opposite his daughter, trying to get her attention. He lost sight of her behind the seats and when he got to the corner she was gone.

The man sitting next to Jack Lynes watched her and said, "You've got that right here on your place. Jesus!"

"That's jail bait, Fossy." Jack smiled weakly at him.

"That's worth six months. Hell, if everybody went to jail who dipped his pen in that inkwell, the county high school wouldn't have a football team, I'd bet on that."

"Stay away from her, Fossy. Don't make trouble." Jack Lynes sighed. The whiskey he had drunk was wearing off, leaving a headache and melancholy. He wished they were all gone. Fossy and Charlotte weren't getting along. Sally Carter was the silly cow her brother Mark had called her and her husband, Bitsy, was a bore. He was tired of these chicken fights. He drained the silver flask and put it back in the pocket of his jacket and closed his eyes.

The fight ended without his noticing. They were scattering sand over the bloody pit. He got up and went around the stands to the toilet. There was a small cabinet in the office where he kept whiskey, and he sat there drinking until he knew he needed fresh air. When he got back to the fights, Fossy Glove was no longer in his seat, and he saw that Bitsy was not there either. Amy Cumberley had moved over across the pit to talk with Mark Nailles and he was alone.

He didn't like it. He knew that Amy had asked Kenyon to invite Mark Nailles to Copperfields that weekend, and Kenyon had refused, as he knew she would. He got up and went outside, taking deep breaths of the cool night air, wondering where Bitsy and Fossy had gone.

When he came back to the pit, most of the people in the upper seats were drifting out. Amy was gone and so was Mark Nailles. It was close to midnight, and the fights were over. He set out to walk up the lane to his house.

Sheriff Rowe worked the crowd outside the barn when the fights broke up. He was unopposed in the upcoming election and it was months away, but it didn't hurt to keep in touch. Most of the cars had driven off when he got into his official car and pointed it down the lane toward the highway. His headlights picked up someone perched on the white rail fence. He slowed as he came up. Peaches Rillbon, in jeans and a ruffled low-cut blouse, waved to him.

He rolled the window down. "Hey, honey, you're out late, aren't you?"

"Just enjoying the pretty night, Sheriff. Too nice to be inside."

"Well, you take care, you hear?" He put the window up and eased down the lane, watching her in the rearview mirror. Somebody is going to enjoy something, it ain't going to be the pretty night.

Peaches sat there until she heard footsteps. She hopped down and waited, then joined the figure who appeared beside her. She giggled but did not object when she felt a hand move across her bottom as she and Bobby Horewood went up the lane toward the barn.

CHAPTER 3

Jeff Rillbon found Mark Nailles's body Saturday morning when he went to get the lawn tractor from the shed attached to the cockfight barn. It sprawled against one wheel, face down; dried blood had turned brown on the tire, the floor, and the red jacket.

Pat Rillbon told his son who the dead man was after Jeff ran back to the house, and the two of them stood looking at the bloody mess. "He used to be a friend of the Lyneses. They grew up together. Go call the sheriff while I go up and tell Jack Lynes what's happened."

Jack Lynes was in the kitchen making Bloody Marys. He had a hideous hangover and the last thing he wanted to do this morning was to knock a little ball over a lot of grass. Maggie Allan was preparing trays for breakfast. Jack had always been slightly afraid of Maggie; less lately, but he had never got over his childhood caution. She had worked for his mother for as long as he could remember, in Richmond, and at Copperfields since he and Kenyon had moved there. He felt that Maggie had some hold over his mother; he knew that she intimidated him. He was sure that she knew more about him than she should and was saving it up to serve some night at dinner.

Pat Rillbon pushed through the kitchen door, stood looking at the two of them. "Jack! Thank God! It's Mark Nailles—something's happened—he's in the tractor shed, all cut up. He's dead."

The tray Jack Lynes held trembled and he put it down before he dropped it. He saw Maggie turn from the table, look at Pat, then go back to her work without a word.

"Jesus! What happened?"

"The blood on him is dried, like he's been there for a while. Jeff's calling the sheriff."

"You're sure it's Nailles? What's he doing in the tractor shed?"

"It's him all right."

Jack Lynes poured more vodka into his tomato juice and drank the whole glassful. "Oh Christ! What a thing to happen! We've got a golf game in two hours."

Maggie followed the two men out of the house. She climbed the stairs to the apartment over the large garage where she lived, went through the living room to the bedroom beyond. She leaned over the bed, shook the shoulder of the woman asleep.

"Serene! Serene, honey. Wake up!"

Her daughter turned over, opened her eyes, looked up sleepily.

"Wake up, honey. I got good news. Somebody has done killed that white son of a bitch."

Angus Bealle had come on at seven and was the only officer on duty in the sheriff's office when the call came. He felt himself sweating as he listened to Jeff, found himself stammering as he asked the wrong questions. "I'll call the sheriff," he promised as he hung up.

Though he had been a deputy for only four months, Angus had always wanted to be a policeman. He couldn't wait until he was old enough to apply for the job; meanwhile he had spent his time reading about police procedure and taking some night courses at the community college in Richmond. It meant driving sixty miles each way twice a week, but he liked doing it. He wanted to be a professional; *some day* he was going to run for sheriff. He knew how incompetent Shad Rowe was, but he also knew how entrenched he was with the county's voters. Angus was prepared to wait and make himself a first-rate policeman.

He had tried to get the sheriff to introduce a standard radio code without success. "Hell, Angus, who wants to mess with all that? Nobody has trouble understanding what I say. I guess you understand me, too, don't you?"

Ethel Sue Shufflet, the part-time Saturday dispatcher, looked at him eagerly. Something big was up, but she couldn't tell what by Angus's questions.

"Man oh man," Angus said. "Somebody's dead out at the Lynes's place, it looks like a killing."

"You want I should call Sheriff Rowe? I know where he is."

"Lord yes, call him."

"He'll eat us alive, Angus. We ain't supposed to know where he is."

"Then call his house. Tell Mrs. Rowe I need him out at the Lynes's place."

"Maybe I can get him on the radio; if he left it on in the car he might hear it through the bedroom window. Irmene says he's done that before; it's so loud it would wake the dead." Irmene was her best friend, and it was Irmene's mother's bedroom.

The barn where the cockfights were held was beside a lane that turned off to the right from the main drive to the Lynes's house. Angus guessed it was no more than a quarter of a mile. The lane continued for several hundred yards beyond the barn, ending at the house where Pat Rillbon and his family lived. The ground fell off behind the barn, and the entrance to the tractor shed, around the corner from the barn doors, was banked to provide a flat ramp.

The tractor shed door was closed when Angus arrived. Pat Rillbon was standing beside it, talking to Jack Lynes. There were two women, four men in a group standing to one side. Angus recognized Mrs. Lynes but did not know the other woman. He had passed two women walking toward the Lynes's house as he drove up the lane.

"Where's the sheriff?" Jack Lynes demanded as Angus got out of his patrol car. "Hasn't he been notified?"

"He's . . . he'll be along. I'm the deputy on duty."

"My God! You're just a boy."

"It's okay, Jack." Pat Rillbon stepped in. "I know him."

"At least you're a policeman. But I want the sheriff here, so we can get this thing cleared up. You're sure you know what to do?"

"Yes, sir," Angus said, knowing he wasn't sure at all. "Just tell me what happened."

Jack pointed to the door, leaving it for Pat Rillbon to take over. Rillbon pulled the door back enough for one person to enter and waited for Angus.

Angus had seen traffic accidents and once he had investigated a shooting at a tavern, but he had never seen a real murder before.

The shed smelled of oil and gasoline, dust and blood. The body lay sprawled on the floor against a wheel of the tractor. The red jacket and the dark green sports shirt were ripped in half a dozen places; blood had dried in wide stains over the shirt and the plaid trousers. The face and hands were black with blood and had been slashed repeatedly with some sharp instrument. Blood matted the hair and the clothes.

Angus took one look at it and backed out of the shed to the open air, where he turned and put one hand against the door to support himself. He felt his face sweating and he fought to keep his stomach from dumping in front of all those people.

Pat Rillbon put a hand on his arm while he got his breath back. Angus let it stay there for a moment then pulled away. "I'd better get back in there." He looked at the people nearby. The men were strangers, except for one of the farmhands he had seen before but did not know. Jeff Rillbon was standing with his mother and his sister well apart from the rest. Jeff had been a year ahead of him in high school, smart as hell, and a good athlete. Best football player the school had. Angus turned to Pat Rillbon. "Tell Jeff not to go anywhere, please. I got to talk to him, seeing he found the body." He took out his notebook. He had to start somewhere.

"What was his—the deceased's name?"

Jack Lynes spoke up. "Nailles. It's Mark Nailles. He was—he was—I've known him all my life."

Kenyon Lynes came toward them. She was wearing a green raincoat over her nightclothes. "Hello. I'm Kenyon Lynes." She held out her hand as though she were receiving him at a party. Her smile welcomed him yet told him she was in charge. Then, dismissing him, she turned to her husband. "Jack, I really think you should get the sheriff here and get this thing settled as quickly as possible. You can't let him lie there like that forever."

"No, ma'am," Angus said. "Nobody can move him yet."

"Then he should be decently covered."

"Sorry, Mrs. Lynes. Nobody ought to touch him until—I say so." The sudden assertion of authority gave Angus courage. "This is a criminal investigation, Mrs. Lynes. I guess you and your friends better go back to your house until we're through here."

Kenyon Lynes started to speak, then stopped and turned to her husband. "Jack, have somebody get in touch with Cap Cumberley. He'll see that something is done. He's the commonwealth's attorney."

"I'll see to that, Mrs. Lynes," Angus said firmly.

"For God's sake, Kenyon, with Amy here?"

"Never mind Amy being here," the dark-haired woman who had been standing with Kenyon Lynes said, moving quickly from where she stood to come across the grass. Her thin tanned face was tense as she pointed directly toward Peaches. "She's responsible for this mess, every bit of it, the predatory little snake. Everybody saw the way she was tossing those girlish charms around the barn last night, at Mark and at every other man in the place."

"Amy, please!" Kenyon said, but the woman brushed her aside.

Peaches glanced around at her mother and brother, then straightened up defiantly. "You can't scare me. I know about you and him, and about some of the others, too."

Amy reached out and seized the neck of Peaches's dress. The fabric ripped, coming off one shoulder and down one arm, exposing her left breast. Peaches spun around, grabbing Amy's arm and pulling her forward. Amy lost her balance and fell to one knee while Peaches leaped at her, pushing her backward and clawing at her face. Before Rillbon and Angus could pull her away, there were bloody scratches down Amy's cheek.

Rillbon held his daughter by the arm as she kicked backward and Angus helped Amy Cumberley rise. She put her hand to her face, looking at the blood on her fingers.

Rillbon pushed Peaches away. "Stop that! Now!" She jerked away, pulling at her torn clothes, and ran toward the house holding her dress over her shoulder. Her mother followed her.

A thin line of blood ran down Amy's cheek and she touched it, looking at her hand. Angus went to his patrol car, found a first-aid kit, and handed her a swab of cotton. She pressed it to her face but waved him away when he produced a vial of Merthiolate. He was anxiously aware that the crowd was watching him.

Amy's anger left her as quickly as it came. "I shouldn't have done that. I lost my temper. But you ought to know something; last night Mark said he was stopping by the house, but when he didn't I walked over to the barn. I didn't see anybody there, but as I was going back to the house I heard somebody walking ahead of me up the lane."

"Did you see who it was?"

"Who else would it be? It was that little tart. I knew it was, when Mark didn't show up. Earlier in the evening he asked me who she was. Knowing Mark—"

Kenyon Lynes came up to Amy. "Let's go back to the house; you're upset. There's nothing we can do here."

"That's a good idea, Mrs. Lynes," Angus said. "If you all go back, it will save a lot of trouble. I'd appreciate it if you'd take the others with you."

Kenyon Lynes nodded, went to say something to her group. After a minute the two women got into her station wagon and drove off. One of the men went with them, the others stayed.

Angus called the office on his radio but Ethel Sue said the sheriff hadn't been home all night. He asked Pat Rillbon where there was a telephone; Rillbon took him into a small office in the barn. He found Cap Cumberley at home.

"This is Angus Bealle, Mr. Cumberley. I'm up at the Lynes's place. I can't get hold of the sheriff, and I've got a dead man on my hands up here. Mrs. Rowe said the sheriff didn't come home last night and she doesn't know where he is."

"What you mean you've got a dead man?"

"You know that barn where they have the fights? There's a dead man in the shed next to it. Cut up pretty bad and been there awhile. Name's Nailles. Mark Nailles." Angus heard Cumberley suck in his breath but said nothing. "Jeff Rillbon came on him this morning. I've only been on the force four months, Mr. Cumberley. This is the first time I've run into something like this. I mean, involving somebody like Mr. Jack Lynes and all."

"What about the other deputies?"

"I'm the only one on duty."

"Have you called Dr. Panthorpe?"

"No sir. Just the sheriff and now you."

"Call him. He's the local medical examiner. Don't move the body until he tells you to and be sure that nobody messes with anything. Have you got a camera?"

"I've got one in my car."

"Take all the pictures you think you need. Don't move anything until Dr. Panthorpe is finished."

Dr. Panthorpe was having his usual breakfast of fried eggs, corn cakes, sausage, and jam when his wife came into the dining room. He had eaten the same breakfast every morning for forty-one years and he weighed two hundred and forty-nine pounds.

"Orland, there's a policeman on the telephone, says he's got to speak to you."

"Didn't you tell him I was busy?"

"It's that young Bealle boy, the middle one. Somebody's been killed out at the Lynes's place."

Dr. Panthorpe folded a corn cake into quarters, put the whole thing into his mouth, and chewed while his wife waited. He did not speak with his mouth full. "He knows better than to call me about accidents. Tell him I'll check with Jepson after he picks up the body."

"It's not an accident, Orland. He says somebody's been murdered."

"What am I supposed to do when some farmhand kills another one? Dammit, can't I enjoy a meal without being pestered like this? Tell him to get the body down to the undertaker's."

"It's not a farmhand, Orland. It's some friend of Jack Lynes. I think you better talk to him."

Panthorpe threw his napkin down and pushed back from the table. Mrs. Panthorpe picked up his plate and took it to the kitchen, knowing he would not eat the eggs. She could hear his heavy voice through the open door as she set about preparing fresh breakfast.

"Yes, Bealle, what is it? . . . Dammit, son, you know what to do. Get the body down to Jepson's. Be sure nobody messes with it . . . No, dammit, I don't want to come all the way out there.

There's nothing I can't do a lot easier at Jepson's . . . You mean he wasn't shot? . . . cut up that bad, eh? . . . You just have Jepson wrap him up and take him in. I'll get to it as soon as I can. I've got other patients, too; live ones, that I want to keep alive."

Mrs. Panthorpe put a fresh plate of eggs in front of him, waited patiently until he put down his knife and fork and pushed his plate away. "Fellow named Nailles found dead in Lynes's barn. Cut up pretty bad, Bealle says. Been there some time. Had a cockfight out there last night, it could have been any of the riffraff that goes to those things."

Panthorpe had no use for cockfighting, not because it was cruel and bloody, but because he knew that men and women did things equally cruel and bloody. "There was a Nailles in my class, turned out to be a damned good surgeon. Kin to the Hounbridges some way or other."

Mrs. Panthorpe nodded. The Hounbridges were kin to her mother's family. "If people would just stay with their own kind, things like this wouldn't happen." People with good blood like the Nailles and the Hounbridges set an example. People who allowed things like this to happen were to be deplored. She concluded that the murderer of Mark Nailles was somebody with bad blood. Her mother had always said that there was bad blood in the Lynes family. Take that dreadful old Fessenden Lynes who had come here and built Copperfields.

CHAPTER 4

Sheriff Rowe opened his eyes to the urgent poking of his bedmate. The light was bright through the open window.

"Shad, can't you do something for Pete's sake about that radio? It's been going on like that for thirty minutes."

"Oh Jesus! I thought I turned it off." He could hear the sound, and he knew it was Ethel Sue, but he couldn't make out the words. He reached for his trousers, being careful with the zipper as he pulled them over his naked bottom, and went barefoot out of the house trailer. As he reached into his car for the microphone, he felt a painful spasm in his back.

"What is it, Ethel Sue?"

"Sheriff, I been trying to get you for the past half hour."

Rowe put a hand on his lower back, pressing at the pain. "You got me now, honey. What the hell do you want?"

"We got a—we got some kind of killing, Angus said I should let you know."

"Dammit, can't he handle it? What is it—a shooting?" Shootings were generally reserved for Saturday nights.

"I don't know yet. We got a call from up at the Lynes's place that somebody's been killed and it ain't no tractor accident."

Rowe rubbed his back. The pain grabbed him as he leaned forward into the automobile. A killing so soon after a cockfight could make trouble, even if the two had nothing to do with each other. "All right, Ethel Sue."

He went back into the house, grimacing with pain. He told the woman what he had heard.

"Oh brother. If it's one of them fancy people up there, you got trouble, Shad."

"What trouble?"

"You get a local killing, you can pretty well find out what's happened because you know what's going on. You take people in those big places, they're different. They got lawyers to look out for them, and they do things and know people you just don't know about. It could get into the papers, and all." She sat up in the rumpled bed not bothering to pull the sheet over her. "Give me a cigarette and hand me that robe. I'll get you some breakfast."

He cried out as he reached for the orange chenille robe on a chair. "It's my goddamn back. I got to get dressed and call Doc Panthorpe. Get him to give me something."

It was more than an hour later when he drove up the lane to Copperfields. Dr. Panthorpe had stuck him with something that killed the pain and told him to go home and go to bed if he knew what was good for him. Rowe promised him he would as soon as he was through at the Lynes's place. Panthorpe told him he'd get over to Jepson's undertaking place and look at Nailles's body as soon as Jepson called him.

Jepson and his assistant were loading the basket into the hearse outside the barn. Rowe eased out of his vehicle carefully and moved sideways toward Angus Bealle. His back hurt less when he moved that way. "Doc Panthorpe should have come out here," he said to the deputy. "But you can't tell him nothing."

"He told me to send the body to Jepson's."

"Just want it understood I had nothing to do with it."

"No, sir. It was me." Angus spoke with a confidence new to him. The morning was beginning to make its mark. "I took pictures of everything before they moved him and I shut up the shed so nobody could mess with things." He handed Rowe a packet of instant photographs. The sheriff shuffled them through his rough fingers. The man was a bloody mess, all right. "Ripped him up something fierce. What the hell did they use, a razor?"

"I don't know yet, Sheriff. Haven't turned up any weapon."

"There's blood all over. Look there, cut him all over his belly. Ripped his pants; tore them clean open. Cut his privates up pretty bad, it looks like."

"Yes, sir."

"You reckon he was trying something funny? Wasn't queer, was he?"

"I don't know. I haven't turned up anything that would tell me."

"And you won't, standing around here like this." He turned and called to Jepson. "Okay, Irby, you can go. Tell Doc Panthorpe to call me when he finds out anything."

"Sure thing, Shad."

Irby was in the hearse beside his assistant when Rowe called out again, crabbed his way to the hearse, and waited for Jepson to roll down the window. "Say, Irby. You get a lot of people in and out of your place. How about doing what you can with these." He handed the undertaker a handful of small cards. "Election coming up. I got to reach everybody I can."

"Sure, Shad." Jepson took the cards, ran the window up, and signaled the driver to move. The cards had a photograph of the sheriff in uniform, a message urging his re-election. Jepson showed them to his assistant then dropped them into a small trash bag. "I'll do what I can." They both laughed.

Rowe returned to Angus. "Let's take a look." He indicated the shed where Jeff had found the body. Angus opened the door and the sheriff peered inside. "This where he was killed?" He pointed to the spot next to the tractor where bloodstains soaked the hard oily dirt floor.

"I can't say, Sheriff."

"This was where they found him?"

"Yes, sir. But he might not have been attacked here. He must have died here, but I don't see where there was much of a fight going on in here."

"Then how the hell did he get in here? Walk on his tippy-toes?"

"He might have been dragged in or crawled from somewhere. With everybody moving around so much I haven't had much chance to check." He had scratched the outline of the body in the dirt floor with a hoe handle before it had been moved. Rowe stared at it and at the pictures in his hand. "In all that scuffed up dirt it don't look like something was dragged in from outside."

Angus had strung orange plastic ribbon around the area outside the shed from the building to a tree and back to the large barn door. Rowe examined the ground around the entrance but the crushed stone showed little evidence of traffic over it. He kicked at a broken whiskey bottle lying in the grass, knocking the largest fragment into the shrubbery.

Angus bent over and pointed. There was a series of small brown stains at the edge where it met the grass. He took out a pocket knife and a small plastic bag.

"What the hell are you doing?"

"It's blood, Sheriff." He lifted the gravel with his knife and dropped it into the bag. The sheriff tried to bend over to look but groaned and backed off.

Angus moved along the grass away from the shed. There was more blood leading around the shed to the back of the barn. Every four feet or so he found another small drop. It followed the retaining wall of the ramp and the edge of the barn wall. At the rear corner where large rocks had been piled to prevent erosion there were larger stains. "He must have stopped here." The land dropped off behind the barn and along the foundation for four or five feet a bed of rock had been spread to stop the washing from rainwater off the roof. At the corner of the barn the trail stopped. "Whoever did it maybe caught him here and he made his way around the barn to the shed."

"Or he was dragged."

"No, sir. There isn't enough blood. This looks like he only had a cut finger or something."

"All right. So he crawled along here—" The sheriff moved back around the barn keeping well off the trail of blood. "And went inside the shed here where he died."

"No, sir. I'd say somebody with a minor cut was back here, either before he attacked Nailles, or after. Or Nailles was back here and got a minor cut and went around to the shed. The murderer could have been chasing him."

"Then they must have met behind here and got into some kind of ruckus."

"That could happen, Sheriff. But it looks like the killing took place in the shed."

"Well somebody was sure as hell back here. You better make up your mind, Bealle, what you think happened. What I think is somebody cut him up in the shed, then went around the shed there and dropped a little blood on the way. He was bleeding some because Nailles got in a lick or two before he was killed."

"Yes, sir. It could be that way."

At the double doors of the cockpit barn Rowe lifted the latch and indicated that Angus was to swing one open. The space inside was dark but Angus made out in the shadows the tiers of seats. "Hey, Sheriff, this is a cockfight pit."

"What the hell you think it was, a whorehouse?" The sheriff found the light switch and put the center of the barn in a fluorescent glow. Dried blood and feathers streaked the sandy floor, and a dead bird, its black and red feathers dulled by death, lay stiff and bloody against a wall. Already there were flies buzzing around its carcass. The smell of men and poultry, dust and feathers oozed out of the doors as the day was admitted.

"You ain't going to get much out of here," Rowe said crossly. "Look at that mess." He pushed the dead bird with his foot, turning it over. It was stiff with rigor mortis, its feathers flat where the body had settled.

Angus moved around the arena while Rowe stood at the doors. On the front row of seats to the left he found blood spattered across the boards and under a seat. Several small feathers hung in the matted blood. He was bending over scraping up blood when Rowe came up behind him. "That's where that chicken flopped over and messed up some of their clothes, whoever was sitting there."

"You think this came from a chicken?"

"Sure it did. But you check it out anyway." Rowe moved carefully along the pit. "Now what I'd say, he had a fight with somebody behind the barn there, then took himself around to that shed. Question is, who'd want to do a thing like that? Seemed like a right fine fellow to me. I won fifty dollars off him." He looked at Angus. "Just a friendly little wager, you understand. Nothing to make something out of."

"Sheriff, you know this is all going to come out, about the cockfighting and the gambling. And the fact that you were here."

"Hell fire, Angus, it was all between friends, you might say, and it was all done in private."

"Was he betting a lot of money?"

"He was having a good time with his money, I'll say that."

"Somebody could have beat him up if he didn't settle up. You think that's possible?"

"Sure it's possible, but you don't cut somebody up like that over fifty dollars."

"How many people were here last night?"

"Must have been fifty, maybe."

"You know who they were?"

"It's not like they let strangers in; it's by invitation, so to speak. Christ, Angus, we can't hunt down everybody that was here. That would take all week. First thing I got to do, I got to talk with whoever it was found him."

"Jeff Rillbon."

"You get him over here. We got to go careful on this. People like this is different from us. With their money and everything. We got to watch how we go about this."

"Somebody killed him, Sheriff. It's our job to find out who did it."

"We'll get him. Comes down to it there ain't but two reasons why people get killed. Money and sex. Sometimes the two is mixed. Sometimes there's no money where there ought to be, or too much where there ought not to be. Or there's too much screwing where there ought to be less. Nobody gets killed because they don't screw around. Comes down to it, that's all there is.

"Now in this case, if it's money, then the dead man owed somebody or somebody owed him. If it's the other, he was tapping something he wasn't supposed to tap. I know one thing, Bealle, people like that ain't going to tell me about it. I only went through the eighth grade."

"We'll do the best we can, Sheriff. I'll go get Jeff Rillbon."

CHAPTER 5

Sheriff Rowe's questioning technique was based on two assumptions: That the person questioned was guilty and that the answers would be lies. He listened to Jeff Rillbon's straightforward report of how he had found Mark Nailles's body with increasing impatience. His painful back did not improve his tolerance.

"I didn't see you around last night."

"I wasn't here last night."

"Pretty much everybody else in your family was. Your pa and your sister."

"I wasn't and my mother wasn't. You could say pretty much everybody wasn't."

"You don't like cockfights?"

"They're cruel and nasty. And against the law."

The sheriff hitched his gun belt impatiently. "They're good enough for your old man, and they're good enough for Jack Lynes, boy." Jeff shrugged. "Where was you last night?"

"I was out with some friends; we went over to Charlottesville."

"You can prove that?"

"Any time, Sheriff."

Rowe turned to his deputy. "You get his statement, then you come over to Mr. Lynes's house."

"I've already got it, Sheriff."

"Then you come along with me. I got to talk to Mr. Lynes and his friends. Just remember we got to do it so we don't get them all upset."

Angus followed the sheriff's car with his own and stopped behind him in the driveway. They were mounting the steps when Kenyon Lynes opened the front door. She had put on a dress and added makeup to her anxious face.

"Sheriff, I think you ought to know there's already been a

reporter calling from Charlottesville. I don't know how he heard about it, but he's called twice. He's on the telephone now."

"Now, Mrs. Lynes, I can't give out no statements on this; you tell him that."

"I'm sorry, Sheriff. I told him you were here and he said he'd wait."

They followed her into the front hall, and Kenyon Lynes indicated a telephone on a table near the stairs. Rowe picked the instrument up as though it were toxic. "Sheriff Rowe . . . I've got nothing to say at this time . . . now you look here, sonny, never mind about that. You'll get a statement when I'm ready . . . You can quote me that I've taken charge of this investigation personally and I'll have something to say when the times comes . . . That's all I've got to say." He put the telephone down hard.

"He asked something I don't know about," Rowe said. "Did the dead man have a family?"

Kenyon looked stricken. "Yes. His wife. They're separated, but she's still his wife. And there's a son."

"His wife wasn't with him?"

"No. No. She lives in Richmond."

"What's the son's name?"

"Broderick. Brod. Somebody must let her know, Sheriff Rowe. She mustn't hear it on the radio or television news."

"I can have the Richmond police let her know."

Kenyon shook her head. "That wouldn't be right. If you wish, I can telephone a friend who knows her, who can go and see her. She mustn't hear this from the police."

"That would be the thing to do, I reckon, if you think so. Then she could tell the boy."

"He's not a boy. He's twenty-two years old. You'll have to do that, Sheriff."

"How'm I going to do that, Mrs. Lynes?"

"You could send your deputy, perhaps. He's been at Sweet Valley since sometime last winter."

"You're telling me, Mrs. Lynes, this boy is one of them over there at that place?"

"I know it sounds unlikely, but he's there."

Rowe shook his head, unbelieving, then turned to Angus. "I'm going to be tied up here, Bealle. You get on over there to Sweet Valley and find him; bring him back here, you understand? Don't waste any time over there."

"Yes, sir."

"You get back, you check with me. And you bring that boy back with you."

"He may not want to come, Sheriff," Kenyon said.

"He'll come if I say so, Mrs. Lynes."

"Unless you want me to arrest him, he doesn't have to come," Angus said.

"I want you to do what I told you, go over there and bring him back here with you." The sheriff was impatient.

Angus nodded and went out of the door. He heard the sheriff ask Mrs. Lynes what a boy like that was doing at a place like Sweet Valley. "He lives there," she said as he closed the front door.

He drove out to the main road, turned east, followed the highway for ten miles, then turned off to a secondary road through woods and open fields. The fields were planted in wheat flourishing in the spring sunshine or were fenced for pasture. The earth in the lower end of the county was not the rich redness of the upper hills; it was paler, with shale and gravel mixed with the loam. The houses were small, some of them shabby, but all of them familiar to Angus, who knew the county as well as he knew his mother's yard. He turned off the macadam onto a dirt and gravel road and at a sign that said SWEET VALLEY turned again between cedar posts and drove through an overgrown field of cedars and underbrush.

The sign was surprisingly elegant for its location. It was large and rectangular, hung from solid posts expertly joined. The sign was deeply carved and skillfully stained, showing curving branches of leaves surrounding graceful letters: SWEET VALLEY PEACE AND FRIENDSHIP.

Beyond the stand of cedars the fields cleared; on one side half a dozen cows grazed behind a wire fence; on the other behind a similar fence two women and a man worked a garden filled with the fresh green of new cabbage, broccoli, peas, and lettuces. A small child waved at Angus as he passed. The adults looked up at

Deadly Nightshed

him and smiled. Angus recognized the man as the one called Rebo, one of the women as Hebe. The child was called Trade.

He could not remember when Sweet Valley had not been there, although he knew that it had been started when he was a small child. It had begun, one of them had told him, in 1966. Angus had heard his parents talk about the hippies who had moved to the old farm, and he grew up seeing them around Phoebeville. By the time he was in high school everybody took them for granted and had generally good things to say about Sweet Valley.

One of the girls in Angus's class had joined them for a few months but after that she had gone to Charlottesville and got a job at a 7-Eleven and married the assistant manager.

Beyond the recently built cattle barn was the old farmhouse, its clapboards left unpainted as new boards were added, but it had no air of dilapidation. It formed one corner of a wide common around which were ranged half a dozen buildings with pitched roofs, clerestory windows, and wide porches. The road ended at the farmhouse.

Angus pulled into a parking space beside a large shed. Its doors opened to the spring day. There was a panel truck backed up to the loading platform, the rental company logo showing through the coat of paint that had been brushed over it. On the side of the van was a smaller version of the sign at the gate.

A man called Vee came out of the shed as Angus got out of his patrol car. His overalls hung loose around his thin waist as though he were standing inside them rather than wearing them. His long hair, thinning on top, was tied behind his ears with a string and his beard came to the bib of his faded overalls. His eyes were astonishing in their blue clearness. The sound of Jethro Tull rocked through the air from a stereo in the shed.

"Hey, man," the bearded man smiled at Angus. A gold earring glinted in the sun. Angus got out of his patrol car and followed the man into the shed. His manner was easy and casual.

Angus stopped by regularly when he was in that part of the county. The members of the community liked him because he was genuinely interested in what they were doing and because they had worked over the years to dispel the idea that Sweet Valley was a weird sort of place.

A lot of it made sense to Angus. He didn't want to live there but what they did they did sensibly. And he usually found Moon there.

The room they entered was large, open on two sides through wide doors. Three rows of rough tables filled the middle of the room, with maybe thirty people working at them. Half a dozen industrial sewing machines were going at one end. The men and women looked up from their work; some of them waved and all of them gave him some sign of recognition. Five of them wore stereo headphones.

"You want some coffee, man?" When Angus nodded, Vee poured coffee from a Mr. Coffee machine on a counter into earthenware mugs and handed him a cup. Angus stirred brown sugar from a bowl into his, poured fresh cream from a pitcher.

The workers kept busy at their tasks. At one table they cut heavy canvas into patterns and stacked the pieces neatly near the machine operators who stitched them together. This was one of the ventures at Sweet Valley that kept them going—a shop that manufactured canvas tote bags, backpacks and duffel bags. They had a silkscreen shop where they produced special order bags for organizations that were politically okay: Health food stores, public radio stations, clean air campaigns, and save the furry animals foundations. Sweet Valley was a going business, its mail-order business was the largest customer at the Phoebeville post office.

Vee was the Alpha, the head of the organization, but he took his turn working in the garden and at the sewing machines. Rebo, who was in the garden today, was head of the business committee. The carved sign at the entrance was a sample of the most recent venture, successfully taking advantage of the fashion for the rustic.

Angus had been stopping by regularly for over two years. When he was working at the courthouse before he had joined the sheriff's force he had met the girl called Moon, a sweet-faced tiny thing. He wasn't sure what he thought of the life at Sweet Valley. Moon tried to explain it to him. "We want to be free to live our own lives. To express ourselves. Sex is just part of it. We don't have to do it if we don't want to, but if two people have a relationship everybody respects it."

"You respect it even when it's two guys?"

"That's their way. You have to respect it."

"I can't do that." They had been talking last winter when he had come by. He liked Moon, liked talking to her. She was smart enough even though some of the things she said didn't make sense to him. Like giving up college to come to Sweet Valley. She had told him very little about herself, not even her real name. "That's all behind me. I'm just Moon. That's all."

"I don't like the idea of you—of you doing it with just anybody."

Moon laughed and touched his hand. "Oh, Angus, it's all right. I don't do it with just anybody. I'm never going to do it again. Ever."

Angus was sorry to hear her say that. "You never know what might happen."

"That's what is so good about Sweet Valley. You can be a part of something but you don't have to get messed up anymore. But I promise you, Angus, if I ever was going to do it again, I'd do it with someone like you."

So Angus kept going back to Sweet Valley. Now he looked about the shop for Moon. She wasn't there.

"Look, Vee. I'm here on what you might call official business today. I'm looking for a fellow named Brod Nailles."

Vee looked at him quickly then down at his cup. "What's he done?"

"He hasn't done anything I know of. I've got some bad news for him."

"Bad news? Hey, man, you can't give Brod no more bad news. He's had his bad news for the week."

"This is something I've got to do. Where is he?"

"Hey, you're the policeman, man. You find him. He hasn't been around here for two days. He cut out last Thursday."

"You know where he went?"

"Nobody knows. Not even his old lady. He borrowed some money from her she'd been saving to go visit her family and cut out." Vee finished his coffee. "What's the bad news Brod needs a policeman to bring?"

"It's his father. His father's dead."

Vee walked to a sink, washed his cup, and hung it on a peg. "I thought you had bad news. For him what you've got is good news."

Angus washed his cup and hung it beside Vee's. "What was the bad news he got?"

"He didn't say. His old lady said he asked her to lend him some money, he had to go see somebody. She didn't ask who."

"Do I know his old lady?"

"Sure. It's Annabel."

Angus knew Annabel. She'd been at Sweet Valley longer than anybody there, and was over thirty years old. One of the children in the commune, a girl about seven, was hers. He had never got to know her, but she struck him as having a knack for mischief. It was just a look she had. She always seemed to be resentful of something.

"Annabel and Brod Nailles—they—?"

"For about three months."

"Can I talk to her?"

"She's not here. She's studying medicine over in Charlottesville. Started last year after she got her degree down in Richmond."

"But she still lives here?"

"Takes the bus over every morning and comes back at night. The company voted to pay for it. It'll be good having our own doctor."

Angus hoped he would never need treatment from her.

CHAPTER 6

Angus drove back to Copperfields. He worried that the sheriff might screw this investigation up. This was something more than a domestic quarrel or a Saturday night brawl. Mark Nailles was from Richmond, with rich connections, murdered in a nasty way while he was visiting his fancy friends. His killer could be one of the people staying at Copperfields, which meant that it could be somebody with as much influence and money as Jack Lynes. He couldn't let Rowe mess this one up, but he didn't know how he could stop him.

Angus wished he knew Mr. Cumberley better. He seemed to be straight, though he kept to himself and didn't talk much. His father had been a fine man; everybody in the county liked him. He had been commonwealth's attorney for more than thirty years before he died the year before. When his son was appointed commonwealth's attorney, folks said it was something the judge owed Cumberley's old man. There had been a lot of talk about Mr. Cumberley, how he had had trouble in Richmond, drinking so much that he had lost his job in his law firm, his wife divorcing him and then his daughter dying. He came back to Phoebeville before his father died to practice law with him. Angus had never seen him anything but sober and he had been helpful and generous with his time whenever Angus had to testify in court. Angus liked Cap Cumberley, trusted him, and wished he could talk to him now.

The sheriff's car was in front of the house when Angus got back to Copperfields. Despite the sheriff's scorn for radio procedure, his patrol car had more antennae than a Russian fishing boat. Jeff Rillbon pulled up behind him in a pickup truck belonging to the farm.

"You got a minute, Angus? There's something—I want to talk to you about something." Angus waited for Jeff to join him. "It's about what happened. It's not going to get my dad in trouble? I mean, when it comes out there was a cockfight here last night. He does it because it's part of his job, you know. For Mr. Lynes."

"I don't know, Jeff. It's been going on a long time, nobody's ever made a complaint."

"They're bound to say they were connected, the fights and that man's death. But maybe they aren't. You have to look at it that way, too."

"I'm sure the sheriff will look into everything, Jeff."

"Hell, Angus, we both know the sheriff can't find the shoes on his feet. I just want you to keep my dad out of it. And my sister too."

"What's Peaches got to do with this business?"

"Nothing, Angus. That's why I don't want her involved."

"You saw what happened this morning."

"That's what I mean. She and Mom had a fight last night and again this morning. Mom didn't want her to go over there, and Peaches said she was going anyway. Dad told her she couldn't, then sent her home when he caught her there. They don't get along very well, Peaches and Mom. I—I guess you know why." Jeff chewed his lip, embarrassed. "She sneaked back out after Dad sent her home. I heard her when she came in. It was late, after I got home."

"What time was that?"

"Around one o'clock."

"Did you see anybody around the barn when you came in?"

"There was a car passed me just before I got to the gates; I think it turned out of here, but I'm not sure. And there was one parked near the corner of the shed. It looked like Bobby Horewood's Camaro."

"Somebody'll have to talk to her, Jeff, after what happened this morning. I'll try to get the sheriff to let me do it. You know who that was she had the fight with?"

"It was Mrs. Cumberley. Mr. Cumberley's ex."

Angus opened his mouth, then closed it. "Jesus!"

"See what I mean, Angus." Jeff climbed into the pickup and drove off.

It was a long minute before Maggie answered the front door and let Angus in. He had never been in a house as large as this one; his parents had a modest brick ranch house which his father, a foreman for the power company, had built on four acres west of Phoebeville. What notions Angus had about how the rich lived were formed from television. From the outside this house promised to fulfill all these notions. It was large, white, with wide windows and spreading wings, surrounded by large trees. Inside it was not slick and shining as he had expected. The hall, though wide, was dark and to Angus's eye rather ugly. There was a large circular table covered in a dark cloth that looked like a rug in the center of the hall; the stairs rose behind some columns to the rear. To the left through wide doors was a square room full of pictures and heavy furniture, and beyond that another room. Matching doors on the right were closed. Maggie hitched her head toward them. "They're in there."

Angus knocked and opened the door. The room was filled with bookshelves in paneled walls. The sheriff was sitting on the edge of a large chair beside a dark mantel opposite the door. The windows were open, white curtains behind heavy draperies billowed into the room with the midday breeze. Angus did not know the man standing near the mantel.

"Yeah, Bealle, what do you want?" the sheriff growled.

"I just want to report I'm back."

"Back from where, for Christ's sake? Where you been?"

"You sent me to Sweet Valley to find the dead—the deceased's son. Don't you remember?"

"Yes, I remember. Did you find him?"

"No, sir. He wasn't there. Nobody knows where he has gone. Been gone since Thursday."

The sheriff winced painfully as he shifted on his cushion. "Well now. How about that? What you been telling me about the boy, Mr. Glove, that's interesting, don't you think?"

"Bears looking into, Sheriff," the man called Glove said. He was tall and thin, his skin boyishly fair and clear beneath his dark hair graying at the temples. "Until you told me, I didn't know precisely where he was. I just knew he and his father had a tremendous quarrel over something last year. I knew the boy had left school, but I didn't know where he went."

"What else did you find out, Bealle?"

"Nobody knows where he went, or why. Two days ago he borrowed some money from the woman he—from a woman at the commune and went off."

"You talk to the woman?"

"No, sir. She's in Charlottesville. She goes to med school there."

"Med school?" Glove's voice was unbelieving. "She lives in some kind of commune and goes to med school?"

"Yes, sir. The commune pays for it."

"Where the hell do they get that kind of money, Sheriff?"

"Ain't like that at all, Mr. Glove. Matter of fact, they got a pretty good operation going over there. They work hard, and they got a good head for business. Make them canvas bags and things they sell in fancy stores in Washington, places like that. Got a good farm going, too."

"Place like that can't do the county any good."

"They don't mean no harm. They keep themselves straight and they bring money in. You can't fault that." The sheriff grimaced a painful smile which he tried to make a sly grin. "What I hear there's a lot of what you might call messing around goes on. They're pretty free with it, you know what I mean."

"Lots of free sack time, eh, Sheriff?"

"Whenever and whatever you want, so I hear."

"It's not like that, sir," Angus spoke up. "They have their own ways but it's not like that. I mean, they're pretty decent people."

"Bealle here keeps an eye on them. Probably gets a little something now and then, too." Rowe turned solemn. "But that ain't our business now. You get a description of the boy?"

"Yes, sir. He's twenty-two, blond hair not too long, about five eight, hundred seventy-five pounds, got a beard, was wearing a T-shirt and jeans, blue running shoes." Angus looked at Glove. "Nobody's allowed to have much money. Most of it goes back into the commune. They can work outside if they want to, to make extra money if they want to go see their folks."

"You mean their families know they're there?"

"Yes, sir. A lot of them come to visit."

"What about this woman he borrowed money from, the one studying medicine?"

"She's older—in her thirties. She's not there, but I've seen her. She's—she's tall and kind of thin, not good-looking."

"You put a bag over her head," the sheriff said. "She's all the same. You put out a notice for the boy, Bealle, see if we can pick him up somewhere. I want to know why he skipped out like that. And you talk to that woman."

"You think he had something to do with his father's death?" Glove asked.

"Never know till we ask." Rowe pushed himself up from the chair. "Jesus Christ, I got to get something for my back. I can't stand this much longer." He moved carefully across the room. "You help me get to my car, Angus."

Angus followed the sheriff out of the house, holding on to the older man as he felt his way down the steps and into his car. "What we got, Bealle, is one kind of a mess. We got to find somebody to pin it on, quick, get this thing cleaned up. It'll be in the newspapers and on the TV. You think this boy could have done it?"

"I don't know, Sheriff. Going off like that doesn't make him guilty."

"Don't make him innocent either. We're dealing with some important people here. Not one of them couldn't make a lot of trouble over this. Got the women all upset."

"Did you get their statements?"

"Didn't write nothing down, if that's what you mean. Talked to them, though. I get the chance I'll put it down."

Angus knew that the sheriff wrote badly and avoided the pencil whenever he could. "You take any notes?"

"I was paying too much attention to what they was saying. I'll remember, you can write it down for me. I want to talk to that Rillbon boy some more. He probably knows more than he's saying. You can learn a hell of a lot by keeping your eyes open, your ears clean, and your mouth shut. Take this crowd. Jack Lynes drinks too much. Been drinking this morning, and he's scared somebody's going to bring up something he don't want to hear. He knows that old business is going to come up. People try to forget things if you don't push them, let it go by. You know why Pat Rillbon's been at Copperfields all these years?"

"No, sir."

"Old Mr. Fess Lynes kept him on here after he got him out of some trouble. He married Selma in spite of the mess she got herself into over at the University. Your daddy never told you?"

"No, sir. He thinks a lot of Mr. Rillbon."

"Hell, so does everybody. He worked for old man Lynes and was going with Selma when they was in high school. Jack Lynes asked her to a dance or something, one of them fraternity parties where they all got drunk and there was a lot of messing around. She got herself hurt. Some say she was ganged by a whole bunch of them fraternity boys. Pat Rillbon went over to Charlottesville after it happened and ended up getting arrested for assault. Old man Lynes got him off and hushed the whole thing up. After she got out of the hospital Selma was in some kind of mental place for almost a year. Then she and Pat got married and old man Lynes gave them a house to live in."

"Jack Lynes did that to her?"

"Him or some of his friends."

"The same friends he's got here now?"

"Don't know about that, but you write their names down and you check them out. You ready? That was Foster Glove in there when you came in. He's a stockbroker. His wife's name is—hell, I forget. Charlotte, Charmaine, something like that. She's a good-looker, but she's a cold one. Then there's Mrs. Mathers, her name is Louise, maybe Lois. She's here but he ain't showed up. Had car trouble, she said. There's a fellow named Barl—spells it like a barrel but calls it Barl—got a funny first name. Biston. They call him Bitsy. Fruity-faced little man. His wife's a sister of the dead man. Her name's Sally Carter. Acted all busted up, but she don't give a fart about him being dead. They both said they got along with the dead man, but this fellow Glove told me Barrell owed Nailles a lot of money. Lynes said it was true, and that the high interest rates was getting to Nailles, he was having some money troubles with some of his real estate developments. Now here's something you can chew on; Cumberley's ex, she and Nailles have been getting it off, the way they talk. She's a tough one, but she's got the look about her. Nailles wasn't the first one and he ain't going to be the last.

"The women came back to the house before the fights was over, except for Mrs. Cumberley. I can certify to that from being there. You heard Mrs. Cumberley say she went back down to the barn later. Glove was the first of the men to get back; he stayed to near the end. Then Lynes and then Barrell. Barrell had to change his clothes because he stood too close to a chicken fight and got blood on his pants. I know that for a fact, I seen him when he done it."

Angus wrote the names in his notebook, cringing as he thought what the sheriff might ask Mr. Cumberley about his ex-wife.

"All the women have been up here for about two weeks. The men came up for the weekend. Seems they always come up here this time of year, to play golf and have some cockfights." He started his car, put it in gear. "Only one I didn't talk to was the cook. You go see if she knows something. Then you call Doc Panthorpe, see what he's found out. He'll have to send the body off for the autopsy, but it don't take no doctor to tell us somebody cut him up something fierce."

"What about the weapon, Sheriff? Did you find out anything about the weapon?"

"Weapon? Christ, Angus, my back's hurting too much to look for no weapon."

CHAPTER 7

Kenyon Lynes opened the door when Angus rang. "Did you find Brod Nailles? How did he take it?" she asked without preamble.

"No, Mrs. Lynes. He hasn't been there for two days. Did you get in touch with his mother?"

"Yes. A friend of mine is at her house now. I told her you were going to see Brod. What do you do now?"

"Put out a notice on him. Maybe he'll get picked up somewhere."

"That sounds so ominous. As though he were guilty of something."

"I didn't mean it that way, Mrs. Lynes. I'd like to talk with your cook now."

"With Maggie? I really don't think she knows anything about this."

"We have to talk to everybody, Mrs. Lynes."

"Yes. I suppose you do." She was wearing a blue cotton dress cut low in a circle over her ample breasts and a cardigan that did not match the dress. She smelled of perfume like fresh fruit, but sweeter. Her hair was no tidier than it had been earlier, and her dress looked as though she had pulled it on in a hurry. One of her tennis shoes had a small hole where a toe had worn through. She's rich, Angus thought, but my mother dresses better than she does. Except that Mrs. Lynes still managed to look rich to him.

"She's preparing lunch now; can't it wait?"

"I'll talk to her in the kitchen, so I won't take up too much of her time. I'd like to ask you some questions first, though."

"I've already talked to the sheriff, Officer."

"Yes, ma'am."

"Then I don't see what else there is to tell you."

"Did you know Mr. Nailles very well?"

"I've known him for years. All my life. He and Jack—Mr. Lynes—were at the University together."

"He was staying here with you?"

"No. He was not staying here." Her tone was emphatic. "It's an awful thing to happen; but I can't say that I'm really sorry that he's dead. Only that it happened here. Mark Nailles was not a very nice person."

"Wasn't he a friend of your husband?"

"Mark Nailles was—he wasn't welcome here anymore. The most complimentary word I can think of to describe him is philanderer."

"I'm sorry, Mrs. Lynes." Angus held his pad and pencil awkwardly. He hated feeling stupid. "How do you spell that?"

She spelled it for him. He'd look it up later.

Kenyon Lynes read his mind. "He chased women as naturally as he breathed, but it was more than that. He had some peculiar preferences; all very ugly." She looked directly at him, almost amused at his innocence. "He liked young girls. God knows that's not confined to him; they all like them young. But Mark was—abominable."

"Yes, ma'am. He and his wife are divorced?"

"Separated. They've been separated for more than five years. She won't divorce him. He's given her plenty of reason. It's so sad for her."

"They told me at Sweet Valley that his son hated him. Is that why?"

"There was so much to hate, I suppose. Mark threatened the boy's mother so badly, and when Brod left the University last year, Mark refused to have anything to do with him."

"Do you think his son could have killed him?"

Kenyon Lynes was silent for a long time. "You might as well know," she said finally. "You'll hear about it sooner or later. About a year ago Mark and Brod had a fight. I don't know what it was about, there were so many things between them. Brod knocked his father about rather badly; Mark's jaw was broken and he was badly bruised."

"Where did this happen?"

"Brod went to Mark's office, pushed his way in. Mark's secretary called the police."

"What business was he in, Mrs. Lynes?"

"Investments in real estate. He started with some property he and his sister, Mrs. Barrell, inherited and built shopping centers and apartments. Jack said he's overextended and has some money troubles. Jack can tell you more about that."

"Did the son go to jail for the assault?"

"No. Mark withdrew the charges. It got in the papers, though."

Angus wrote it down carefully. She was looking at him straightforwardly, taking in his whole body. "Are you new on the force?"

"I've been a deputy about four months."

"I must say you're much more attractive than the sheriff." She moved past him and her elbow touched his arm. As she did, Amy Cumberley came down the stairs. She had a bundle of clothes in her arms.

"I've been trying, Kenyon, but I suppose there's nothing I can do to get these clean."

Kenyon reached out and took the rolled-up garments. "Here, let me get Maggie to try. She's a genius at things like that. Poor Bitsy had to throw his trousers away."

Amy looked at Angus and smiled. "I'm sorry I made such a fool of myself this morning, Officer. I don't usually lose my temper like that." She went through the hall into an adjoining room.

Angus followed Kenyon through the house to the kitchen. Her appraisal of his own body still hung between them. He wondered if all rich women acted like that.

Maggie gave them a quick glance and went on slicing tomatoes. "Can't talk to anybody now, Miss Kenyon. I got five people to feed. You know that."

"I won't interrupt you," Angus said. "I'll just talk to you while you work." Kenyon Lynes went out without saying anything more.

"I'll save you the trouble," Maggie said. "I didn't see nothing, I didn't hear nothing, I don't know nothing. If you want to talk about the weather, I ain't got time."

"You can tell me your name, can't you?"

"It's Maggie. Maggie Allan. With two *a*'s." She picked up some eggs, broke them into a bowl, and began beating.

"How old are you, Mrs. Allan?"

She put her beater down and looked hard at him. "What's my age got to do with anything? I'm old enough to mind my own business, that's how old I am."

"It's just for the record."

"You don't need no record on me. I told you I don't know anything."

"You were here last night?"

"I was in my room asleep was where I was. You don't catch me going to no chicken fight. Those chickens so tough you can't even boil them."

"Did you see or hear anything unusual?"

"First thing I heard was when he came in my kitchen this morning to tell Mr. Jack somebody was dead. I heard plenty after that, the way everybody was carrying on."

"Is your room in the house here?"

"I got an apartment over the garage."

"Anybody else live out there?"

"Nobody. I don't want nobody around on my own time."

"You were by yourself last night, then?"

"I didn't say so, did I?"

"No, you didn't. Were you by yourself?"

Maggie poured oil in the bowl, shook seasoning from a jar, and stirred. "My daughter was with me," she said reluctantly. "She don't live here, you understand. She's visiting me for a few days." She waved her spoon at him. "She don't know nothing about it either, you better understand that."

"Did you know the deceased—Mark Nailles?"

"Of course I knew him. Him and Mr. Jack grew up together. They were friends when they were boys."

"And they are still friends?"

"They been in business together, so you could say they were. He don't come to the house anymore."

"Why is that?"

"I don't ask who Miss Kenyon asks to her house, or why not. He just don't come."

"What is your daughter's name?"

"You don't have to know her name, Officer. She's not in this mess, so she don't have to have her name in it."

"I have to ask, Mrs. Allan."

"But you don't have to know." There was a silence while Angus waited for her to continue. "She came down here from New York yesterday. It won't do her no good to have her name get connected with somebody like him."

"Did your daughter know him?"

Another silence. "Long time ago. I told you, him and Mr. Jack been friends all their lives. But she ain't seen him in a long time, not since she went away. Maybe she saw him around Mr. Jack's house sometime when she came to visit me, but that's all."

"How old is your daughter, Mrs. Allan?"

"She's thirty some, but she don't look it."

"Can you tell me anything else about Mr. Nailles?"

"Yes, sir, there's something else I can tell you. It's good riddance, that's what I can tell you." She spoke with such vehemence that it made Angus laugh. She caught his laughter and threw it back at him with a sardonic smile.

"Look, Officer. You got a job to do just like I do. I ain't being rough on you. You had lunch yet?"

Angus shook his head. He was getting hungry as he watched her work, wondering when he might have a chance for lunch.

"You come back after I get all these ladies fed, I'll fix you something."

"Thanks, Mrs. Allan. I'd like to."

"You can come back by the kitchen door."

"You said you were fixing lunch for five. There's more than that here. I count eight."

"The men ain't eating. They gone off to play golf."

"After what happened?"

"Like Mr. Glove said, he ain't never let Mr. Nailles put him off his game; there's no reason to start now."

CHAPTER 8

Jack Lynes, Foster Glove, and Biston Barrell were putting their golf clubs into the back of a station wagon when Angus went by. He did not recognize the fourth man with them. He was tall and thin, his skin tanned and leathery under his cotton hat. All four wore the rainbow of colors that golfers affected.

"Well, Officer—Bealle, isn't it—Bealle," Jack Lynes said. "You've got good news for us?" His eyes were hidden behind dark glasses which did not conceal his drink-puffed skin. His breath smelled of gin.

"No, sir, Mr. Lynes."

"You ought to get this thing settled," Barrell said. "It's a hell of a thing. There are people who think one of us might have done it."

"Maybe one of us did do it." This from Glove. "We've had good reason, from time to time." He waved a hand around the circle. "We can all remember things about Mark Nailles that would make us want to wish him dead."

"Cut it out, Fossy," the tall man said. "Don't drag all that up again."

"You're Mr. Mathers?" Angus asked.

"That's me. Why?"

"I'd like to talk to you, sir. It'll just take a few minutes."

Jack Lynes looked at his watch. "We haven't got much time, Nick. We ought to get rolling."

"Hell, Jack, the officer's got a job to do," Glove said. "Besides, I'd like to hear where Nick was last night, myself."

"You already know," Mathers said.

"Know where you said you were, old fellow."

Mathers walked away from them, around Angus's patrol car. Angus followed. They stood beside the trunk.

"Okay, Officer, what do you want to know?"

"I understand that you telephoned that you had car trouble last night and couldn't get to Mr. Lynes's house."

"That's right. Had a busted fan belt on my way up. Weren't any garages open, so nothing I could do but spend the night. At a rotten little crib at Bunts Crossroads. But it was clean."

"You know the name of the motel, Mr. Mathers?"

"There's not but one, Officer. It's just behind the Gulf station on the left coming this way."

"Yes, sir. What time did this happen?"

"Oh, maybe seven, eight. Hell, I don't know for sure. I'm bad about times."

"I can verify it with the motel owner."

"You're saying you don't take my word for it? I told you I'm terrible about time. Always was."

"It's routine to verify things like that, Mr. Mathers. You didn't ask somebody to come pick you up?"

"I didn't see any point in messing up everybody's evening."

"You get the fan belt fixed this morning?"

"Soon as they could get a mechanic."

"What time was that?"

"Oh, hell—first thing. Eight—nine maybe."

"Then you drove on to Mr. Lynes's?"

"Got here sometime midmorning. Maybe it was later. I don't know. I never know what time it is. Matter of fact, I just got here a short time ago."

"Are you always vague about time, Mr. Mathers?"

"You think I'm lying to you?"

Angus looked down at his pad then straight at Mathers. "I think you are, Mr. Mathers."

"About what, for God's sake?"

"About staying at that motel. I was by there about three weeks ago, the place is shut down. The owner died last March."

Mathers shifted his hat on his forehead. "Oh Christ!"

Angus waited.

"Tell you what, Sheriff—"

"I'm not the sheriff, sir."

"Then you ought to be. I can see you know your job." He looked toward the station wagon where Glove caught his glance and called out. Mathers answered. "Jack, you guys go on. Don't wait for me. I'll come along later."

"Christ's sake, Nick. He going to arrest you?"

"It's okay, Fossy. I'll be here for a while. Go on, I'll catch up."

The three men got into the station wagon and Jack Lynes drove off down the lane.

"Look here, Officer. I've got myself in a kind of a mess. It's nothing to do with killing Mark Nailles, I swear to you. I'd appreciate it if you could let what I said go for what happened. You're doing your job and it looks like a bang-up one. If there was anything I could tell you that would help you find out who killed Mark, I'd do it. I swear I would. But this mess, it's not—it's got to do with my wife—with Mrs. Mathers and me. She knows damn well I wasn't at that motel last night. I didn't leave Richmond until this morning."

"You can verify that?"

"You see, that's part of the problem. If I can get it verified, can you keep a person's name out of it?"

"I can't promise a thing like that."

"I don't want this person's name messed up in this any more than it has to be. For Christ's sake, man, she's—" He stopped and rubbed his face with his hand. "Holy Christ! How did I ever get involved in a mess like this?"

"I don't know, sir."

"She's—she's still married. They've been separated for years but they're not divorced. That's what I meant. That's all I meant."

"I've got to have her name, Mr. Mathers."

"Suppose I don't give it to you?"

"I guess we can find out some way. And you might be charged with withholding evidence in a capital crime."

"But it's not evidence! She was going to divorce him and I was going to work something out with Lois—Mrs. Mathers. Now this thing has to happen. Jesus! I had to drive up here and pretend that nothing had happened, that I didn't even know—" He stopped, his face draining pale under his tan.

"You knew about Nailles's murder before you left Richmond?"

"It was on the radio. Driving up. On the radio." Mathers was beginning to sweat.

"Mr. Mathers, all I wanted to know was where you were last night. All you had to tell me was you were in Richmond and verify it. You keep trying to lie to me. You were with a woman and you heard about Nailles before you left. It wasn't on the radio. Nobody in Richmond knew about it, except Mrs. Lynes called a friend to go tell Mrs. Nailles."

"Word like that gets around fast. Maybe that was the way I heard it; maybe it wasn't on the radio. Probably some friend of hers told her and she told me. You know how word like that gets around."

"What was her name, Mr. Mathers?"

"I can't tell you. You don't understand."

"Was it Mark Nailles's wife?"

Nick Mathers's tall frame seemed to fold inside his bright shirt; his body shrank and his head dropped on his wide shoulders. Angus thought the man was going to cry. "I swear to you she doesn't have anything to do with this. Can't you leave her alone? She's gone through hell already."

"All I want is for her to verify that you were there."

Mathers pulled at his fingers, removing invisible gloves, looking at his hands as they moved over each other. "It won't do any good to ask her. I won't ask her to lie for me. I do my own lying, but I don't ask anybody else to lie for me. Fact is, I didn't get to her house last night until after eleven. I had—had some other things to attend to. Christ! Everything I say gets me deeper into a hole, doesn't it? Now you'll want to know where I was."

"Best we can tell, Mark Nailles was killed maybe some time after eleven. No need for you to lie about anything."

"You think I'm some kind of a bastard, having an affair like this and lying to my wife. You start lying to cover up and you keep on lying even when you can't. It was that that broke up my first marriage, that and the fact that I never seem to be able to keep away from—other women. I was lying to my first wife about Lois—Mrs. Mathers—even after she knew. I've been seeing this—lady—"

"Mrs. Nailles?"

"—this lady, for over a year now. Mark Nailles was a rotten

son of a bitch, even among the rotten sons of bitches who were his friends. That includes me. I wanted her to divorce him but she wouldn't. She said she wasn't going to let him put anybody else through what she had been through. If he tried to divorce her she told him she'd put his whole life out on the table from A to Z. She'd destroy him."

"Would she have reason to kill him?"

"She had every reason to wish him dead; killing him, no. She didn't. She was in Richmond." He shook his head. "Bastard that he was, you can't believe that people you know, people you went to St. Christopher's School with, would kill somebody."

"Do you know his son?"

"Brod? Sure. You don't think he did it?" Angus did not answer. "He's got reason enough, God knows. That fight last year. It was in the papers!" Mathers rubbed his face. "There was a lot of talk but nobody really knew what happened, except that it was over a woman. Friend of Brod's, they said. Nailles—he couldn't leave them alone. Young girls. Not children, I don't mean that. Young women, eighteen, nineteen. Something about him, they seemed to go for him. He could be very attractive you know. He was funny, a lot of laughs, except when he got off on all that rotten racist crap. I mean, I'm no liberal myself, but he made a big show of giving money to the Klan, things like that. Keep him off the blacks and the Jews, sometimes he could be a real charmer. Especially with women. In the end, though, he always treated them badly. Sometimes I think he put them in a class with all the others he hated. But women seem to like to be mistreated. I don't understand, but there it was." He drew a deep breath and blew it out.

"I have to have an address and telephone number, sir. Where we can reach you."

Mathers gave them to him. "You still have to talk to Mrs. Nailles?"

"Someone will have to, sir."

"I know for a fact she hasn't seen him in over a year."

"If you don't tell me where she lives, I can get it from someone else."

"Okay. Okay." He gave it reluctantly. "You don't know what

kind of a bastard Nailles was. I suppose you know about that business at his fraternity house when he was in college?"

"I'm trying to find out all I can."

"They tried to shut it up but everybody knew about it, even up at Princeton where I was. There was this girl there for a weekend. They'd all been drinking for a couple of days. She wasn't there with Mark, but there was a party, three or four of Mark's friends and the girl. She ended up in a hospital with some bad bruises, somebody said some cigarette burns. They kept her name out of the papers and there was some kind of settlement. It was a nasty business, but there never was any real trouble. I mean, nobody went to jail. Just a rotten stink in the newspaper." He paused. "Mark hasn't changed much; he's just meaner now. You should talk to Amy Cumberley. They've been going together for a while. Two of a kind, if you ask me."

"Yes, sir."

"Ask Lois—Mrs. Mathers—about Amy. Women like to spread that kind of talk."

Angus closed his notebook and put away his pencil.

"Is that all? You're not going to arrest me?" Mathers tried to make light of it but saw he had failed. "I'm sorry I wasn't straight with you. I've been covering my tracks so long, one way or another. I suppose you'll tell my wife what I told you."

"No, sir."

"Then I had better do it. She's got to know, if she doesn't know already." He walked around the patrol car toward the house.

"What about your golf game?"

"How the hell can I play golf now? I've got to talk to Lois before I lose all my nerve."

CHAPTER 9

The plastic ribbon he had strung around the barn flashed orange in the sunshine. Angus ducked under it and undid the seal on the door of the shed. The double doors had a simple wooden bar that dropped into metal brackets to close it from the outside. There was no lock. Too many people had been inside that morning, too many shoes had scuffed the dirt floor for him to read anything from it. Years of dripping oil, tractor wheels, and heavy boots had packed the soil down to a hardpan. The tractor made no tracks when it was driven in and out.

Angus walked around it, carefully avoiding the outline where the body had lain. He scanned the crude shelves along the rear wall. Cases of lubricating oil, a hand scythe, mason jars of assorted nails and screws; a ten-year-old calendar with a picture of a naked woman, her pink breasts pointing high, advertising a farm machinery company. Two used automobile tires hung from a bracket high on the wall above a metal toolbox. Three long-handled shovels, one with a split handle, leaned against the wall. Beside them was an ax and a plastic garbage can with no lid. At the bottom of the can were three empty quart containers for lubricating oil.

Using his handkerchief to cover his fingers, Angus opened the toolbox. Socket wrenches, mechanics' tools, some screwdrivers, all clean and in order. He picked up the ax; there was a film of rust along the cutting edge and dust on the handle. A cobweb pulled away as he lifted it. The blades of the shovels were shiny from use, the handles worn smooth. A downy feather was caught in the broken handle but it had been there a long time. There were no bloodstains on any of the tools.

Angus searched the shed carefully. There were feathers caught in old cobwebs and dust on the shelves, but nowhere did he find anything that might have been used as a weapon to kill Mark Nailles.

The doors to the cockfighting barn were more elaborate than those of the shed; they were double, opening out on heavy hinges and secured with a metal bar and padlock. There was a small door to the left of the larger entrance, with a doorknob and a Yale lock. Angus let himself in through the large door and found the light switches. One threw the fluorescent glare over the center of the room; the other put the softer glow of incandescence over the rows of seats. The walls of the room had been finished in vertical pine boards turned dark by varnish, tobacco smoke, and time. The pit was at ground level, its arena marked only by the rows of seats. On opposite sides of the pit the seats rose almost to the ceiling. The worn blue plush of the old theater seats gave the room a disheveled look; some were down, others pushed up where the spectators had left them. Angus counted the seats: Fourteen in each row, seven rows on each side. Seats for almost two hundred. The barn smelled like a chicken house, of blood, feathers, and the ammonia of chicken dung.

Angus went over the scratched and scrambled sand in the pit for anything that might help him know what had happened. All he could see was that male birds, born to fight, had scratched and cut and pecked, bled and died, casting a dross of feathers on the sand, spilling eyes and blood. He found nothing that told him who had killed Mark Nailles, or how, or why.

He climbed to the third row of seats and moved along it. There was a litter of cigarette butts, gum wrappers, match folders. Under the higher seats he found some candy wrappers, more cigarette butts, peanut shells, three empty pint whiskey bottles, several dozen Coke and Pepsi cans, and an unopened package of condoms. There went somebody's weekend.

In a smaller pit in a room at the far end of the barn he poked through the litter of sand and feathers but found nothing helpful.

He turned the lights out and pushed the doors shut. It was good to be in the sunshine after the closed-up stink of the barn. He was at his car when Peaches called to him as she strolled slowly around the corner of the shed. She had changed to brief shorts and a shirt tied at her waist showing a band of flesh and the dimple of her navel. One button kept the shirt from spilling her breasts. She held her hands behind her back as she called to him.

"Oh. Peaches. I didn't see you standing there. What are you doing by that shed? You ought to keep away from there."

"I want you to arrest her for what she did. You ever see anything like that in your life?"

"You'll have to swear out a warrant first."

"If I was to sue her, I could get a lot of money out of her. She had no right to do that."

"You ought to stay away from here, you know."

"I didn't go inside the strings. Have you found out who did it yet?" She came toward him, her hands behind her.

"We've only just started."

"Well, I found something that might help." She stopped a few feet from him. She was enjoying the effect she was having.

"What's that you've got behind your back?"

"Something you'd like to have, Angus. I mean, besides something I've got you've always wanted."

"Cut out that talk. If you've found something, I ought to know about it."

"If I show it to you, will you do me a favor?"

"I'm a police officer, Peaches. If you've got something to show me—"

"Why don't you come and get it. Try to take it away from me."

"Peaches!"

"Oh all right." She dropped her seductive teasing. "If I show it to you, will you leave my family alone? Jeff didn't have anything to do with it and neither did my father. You know that."

"I don't know anything yet. What is it you've got?"

She brought her hands from behind her and held out her right hand. In it was a small hatchet with a short wooden handle. "I found this behind the shed this morning, before you got here."

"What is it?"

"Look at it, Angus."

He took out his handkerchief and reached for the hatchet.

The blade was blotted over with dark brown splotches like thick rust. "You should have left this where you found it. Now you've had your hands all over it, you messed up any evidence there might be on it."

"You don't have to act so hateful. I thought you'd be glad I found it."

He went to the trunk of his car, found a plastic bag, dropped the tool inside, and locked the trunk. "Okay. Now you show me where you found it."

She led him around the corner to the shed. At the far corner of the barn, beyond the spot where he and the sheriff had searched earlier, a whitewashed fence marked the boundary of the pasture beyond. "It was right here," she said, pointing to the rocky ground at the corner where the fence and barn met.

"What were you doing here?"

"What's that got to do with anything?"

"You shouldn't have been back here; that's what those tapes are for."

"It was before you put the stupid tapes there; besides, I was looking for something."

"Looking for what?"

"Something—I might have dropped. Last night." She said it reluctantly.

"You were out here last night? What were you doing here?"

"What do people usually do behind a barn in the dark, Angus?"

"Oh quit that, Peaches. Who were you with?"

"I'm not going to tell you. It's not any of your business."

"Everything is my business when there's been a murder."

"It didn't have anything to do with any murder."

"It could. You might have seen something, or somebody."

"It was dark. We could feel, but we couldn't see." She giggled.

"What time was that?"

"While the fights were still going on. That was before he was killed."

"How do you know when he was killed?"

"Because—I'm not going to tell you. Not unless you promise something."

"Promise what?"

"To keep my father and Jeff out of it. They don't have anything to do with it, and you know it."

"That's what Jeff said to me earlier about you. Why would he do that?"

"Because he's my brother," she said angrily. "Because he doesn't want you to treat me like a common criminal, that's why."

"Are you a criminal, Peaches?"

"No, I'm not. Neither is my brother. Or my father. You just leave my family alone, you hear me?" She turned and ran across the rocky ground toward the corner of the barn. Angus followed, caught her by the arm as she tripped on a large rock. He held her tightly. "You look here, Peaches. I can put you in jail for withholding evidence. Do you understand that? I want to know who you were with last night, and what you were looking for this morning."

Peaches tried to pull away, but he held her firmly. When she saw that she could not get free, she stopped struggling. "All right then. Turn me loose, and I'll tell you. But you've got to promise not to tell my father."

"I can't promise that, but I won't say anything unless I have to."

"All right then. Turn me loose." She stood rubbing her arm where Angus had held her. "Daddy will kill me if he finds out. It'll be your fault, Angus."

"Tell me who it was, Peaches."

"It—it was him."

"Who is him?"

"Him—the one who was killed. Mr. Nailles."

"You—you were back here with the—with him last night? For God's sake, Peaches. You said it didn't have anything to do with his murder."

"It didn't. I didn't kill him. I was just talking to him outside, and he suggested we take a little walk. That's all. He was very nice. He really didn't try anything very much."

"You should have told me."

"It wasn't that he didn't want to try something, I could tell. It was that somebody came poking around while we were there and he said if she knew we were there she'd raise all kinds of hell. He meant her. Mrs. Cumberley. He said he'd see me again today maybe."

"Was it Mrs. Cumberley?"

She shook her head. "It was too dark to see who it was." She had inched away from him as she talked, and now she turned and backed rapidly away. "Now, you promised, Angus. You leave my family alone, you hear?" She ran around the shed and down the road toward her house.

Angus watched her go and flushed slightly as he realized he was paying more attention to the tight seam of her shorts than he was to what she had told him.

He remembered his senior year in high school. She was a freshman. After a basketball game seven of them had piled into Petey Jackens's car and driven home from Orange. They had been laughing and cheering because Bushanna High had beat Orange, and there was lots of shifting around and settling down for the ride home. Rick Thadd, Betty Flommer, Angus, and Peaches were squeezed into the backseat. Angus sat with his back against the door, Peaches pressed beside him, their down jackets piled on their laps.

He was sharply aware of his knees against her thighs; she shifted and lifted one leg over his knee. She and Betty Flommer were singing some silly song when Angus felt Peaches's hand under the jacket moving up his thigh. She seemed engrossed in the silly lyrics, paying no attention to him as he had to shift his position.

He was terrified. Betty and Rick were bound to notice. She was leaning forward to hear something that Chickie Cannester in the front seat was saying when Angus pushed her hand roughly away. He sat flushed with shame and excitement as she turned her back to him. He knew from the way Peaches was giggling that she knew what she had made him do.

He was inside his patrol car before he realized that he had not found out what it was that Peaches was looking for behind the barn.

CHAPTER 10

Through the shrubbery that screened the garage court from the terrace Angus heard the clinking of tableware and the sound of women's voices. Mrs. Lynes's guests were having luncheon. From the kitchen table a woman looked up as he entered. She was drinking tea from a cup and eating an apple. Her white teeth flashed against her sepia skin as she smiled at him; Angus was struck by the size and whiteness of her eyes surrounding dark pupils.

Maggie was at the sink by the window. "This is the policeman I was telling you about," she said without turning around. "Told him I'd give him something to eat."

The woman at the table held out her hand. "Hello. I'm Serene Allan."

Angus took her hand. "Angus Bealle."

"Mama's been telling me about you, Officer Bealle. You don't look so young as she said."

"If he was any younger he wouldn't be a policeman. That's a fact." Maggie brought a plate to the table. A bed of lettuce supported tomatoes, carrots, two sandwiches. "You better eat something more than that apple, honey. You need to put on weight, you do."

"No thanks, Mama. You know who did this terrible thing yet, Officer Bealle?"

"No, ma'am. Not yet." Maggie put a glass of tea beside his plate.

"I suppose this is just another day in the life of a policeman."

"No. It's my first. First murder. I mean, we had a case last month, a woman shot her husband, but she called up and said she had done it, he was beating up on her something bad." Serene was leaning across the table, almost as though she were trying to hypnotize him. He looked down, picked up a sand-wich. "You know the dead man, Miss Allan?"

Serene dropped her gaze, picked up the paring knife, and cut hard through her apple. The interest in her face was gone, replaced by a shadow. "I know who he is—was. Mama worked for the Lyneses since before I was born, so I know who a lot of their friends are."

"The way Mrs. Lynes talked, he's not much of a friend any-more."

"That may be. I couldn't say." She bit into her apple slice. "He's nothing to me, anyway. Good riddance from all I hear."

"What did you hear?"

Maggie came to the table wiping her hands. "Nobody's going to tell what they hear in my kitchen. Whatever you heard ain't got nothing to do with this. I can tell you that."

"Oh, Mama. Officer Bealle's just doing his duty." She finished the apple and put the peel on her plate. "I'll tell you what I know. Mark Nailles was a slimy no-good bastard. Not techni-cally, you understand. His parents and grandparents have been married for generations. He's got two signers of the Declaration of Independence in his family, but that doesn't keep him from being a bastard. Ask anybody. Ask the Lyneses. You remember, Mama, when he was staying with them and fell off the roof and broke both arms?"

"Hush up, Serene. That was a long time ago." But Maggie smiled through her reprimand.

"Jack Lynes's mother was real sick, when he was about four-teen. She had a nurse to take care of her; the nurse was young and good-looking, and Mark Nailles climbed on the roof outside her bathroom to spy on her while she was taking a bath. He fell off and broke both arms. It would have been better if he had broken his goddamn neck."

"Mrs. Lynes called him a—" Angus took out his notebook and looked for the word. "—a phil-anderer. That means he chased women a lot."

"Chased women? He'd chase a doorknob if it was young enough and had the right equipment. He's a satyr, and satyrs love their nymphs."

"Serene, stop talking that way. It ain't decent."

"It's the truth, Mama. You know it. And I sure know it."

"Serene, you hush!" Maggie picked up a tray and went out through the dining room.

"No, Mama. It's the truth and he ought to know it. Mark Nailles is seven years older than I am. That makes him forty-five. When I was sixteen, the son of a bitch raped me." Serene stabbed at what was left of her apple with her knife, her anger making the plate jump. The word and the gesture lay between them. "I see what you're thinking." She laughed sourly. "If you're going to be a policeman, Mr. Bealle, you're going to have to learn to hide what you're thinking. You're thinking I must have done something to make him do it. That's what men always think, isn't it?"

Angus shook his head. "I was thinking his son is twenty-two, he must have been a married man then."

"He was a married man, Mr. Bealle. With a pregnant wife, who was pregnant when they got married. That's one he didn't get away with."

"What about since then? Did you see him last night?"

As he asked the question, Maggie came back into the room, her tray full of dishes. "You've asked enough questions, Officer. Serene doesn't have to answer any questions she don't want to."

"Never mind, Mama. He's going to find out some way. Yes. I saw him last night. I was taking a walk because it was such a pleasant evening. I walked down the lane to the barn. There was a woman with him, that Mrs. Cumberley. Even though he was a lot older since I had last seen him, I knew who he was. A face like that doesn't change. When I passed he said, 'Hey, don't I know you from somewhere?' and then he said, 'Sure, you're Maggie's daughter. That's who you are. It's been a long time, hasn't it?' I said 'Not long enough.' I didn't want to be anywhere near him. As I walked away I heard the woman with him ask him how he knew me, and he said, 'She's just the nigger gal whose mother works for Jack Lynes.' "

With a sudden fierce movement she stabbed the knife into the table; the blade snapped and dropped to the floor. Serene's fist struck the table and she cried out in pain. She put her bruised fist against her mouth, sobbing. "Just a nigger gal. That's all. Just a nigger gal."

"Hush, Serene! It's all done with now."

"It will never be done with and you know it, Mama. I'll tell you something, Mr. Bealle." She stretched her arm out across the table, her long fingers spread. "You see that? You see what color I am? It wasn't my black grandmother who gave me my light skin. It was some white son of a bitch."

"Serene! You got to stop talking like that!" A buzzer sounded in the room. "I got to go see to Miss Kenyon's lunch, but you got to stop that talk."

"Go on, Mama. Wait on the white ladies. And when one of them acts like she doesn't know you're there, you can just look her in the eyes and tell her to cut out that crap, because her husband's sister is sitting in the kitchen telling a policeman all about it."

Maggie's arm swung in a wide arc and the force of her blow threw Serene's head to one side. The red prints of four fingers rose against her cheek. Serene did not touch her face or lift her head but stared straight at Angus.

He shifted in his seat, pushed his plate back, and then pulled it forward. His face was sweating.

"Slapping me doesn't change things, Mama. The white blood's still there." She put her hand to her cheek feeling the reddening bruise with the tips of her fingers. "You never hit me before in my life, Mama."

"I never had no cause before."

"What's different about now? You know it's the truth and you know I know it."

"He's a policeman, don't you know that?"

"I'm looking for a killer, Mrs. Allan. I've got to ask questions."

"You got to ask questions but you don't have to have the answers to questions you don't ask." Maggie wiped her hands on a towel and moved across the room. "I already told you we don't know nothing about what happened here last night." She went out through the swinging doors.

"You want to know which one of them it is, Mr. Bealle?" Serene spoke through the hand resting against her face. "She's sitting out there eating Mama's food and smiling at Mama when she passes the asparagus. No thank you, Maggie, thank you, Maggie. It makes me want to puke."

"I have to know what happened last night."

"What happened was somebody had put up with all she was going to from Mark Nailles and she killed him."

"She? What makes you think it was a woman?"

"Because it was women he treated the way he did. The men don't give a damn how he acts. They'd be just like him if they had the guts."

"It could have been somebody—a man—who didn't like what he had done to somebody—a woman—he cared about. It could have been that way."

"Maybe it could. But I don't see anybody in this house who cares that much. If there was any kind of justice in this screwed-up world, whoever did it would get a trip to the White House instead of to the Jail House."

"Did you go to the cockfights?"

Serene picked up what was left of the apple, turned it over, and put the wedge back down. "Yes. I was there. I thought it would be something to tell my friends in New York about. I went over to the barn but I didn't stay very long. I didn't even sit down."

"What time was that?"

"It was after ten o'clock. I don't know exactly."

"Did anybody see you there?"

"If they looked at me they saw me. I told you Mark Nailles and Mrs. Cumberley saw me. Mrs. Lynes passed me in her station wagon while I was going down there. She had somebody else with her. The white folks from the big house." She picked up the plate with the bits of apple, stood up, and carried it to the sink. "Look here, Officer. You forget what I said earlier. I was out of line talking about Mama like that. It wasn't her fault. She was right to slap me."

"Can I ask you something about—about the deceased?"

"I've already told you too much, I think." She stood at the sink, put her head back, lifted her face, and smiled at him. It was a model's smile, professional; her whole body was a model's pose, carefully studied. "You think I'm attractive?"

"Sure. Sure you are."

"I made you blush. You're sweet, you know. I really mean it. I never made a man blush before. The kind of men I know couldn't blush for shame because they don't have any; if I asked them if I was attractive they'd have the sheets pulled back before they could answer, then half of them would be in bed with each other. How long have you been a policeman?"

"About four months."

"You like being a policeman? You like poking into people's lives, finding out their dirty little secrets, writing them all down in your little book?"

"It's not like that. This is the first time we've had a real murder in the county since I can remember. Other than a shooting, I mean."

"Shootings don't count, for God's sake?"

"Mostly it's somebody shooting somebody, a husband or one like that, and we know who did it right away."

"And jailing the niggers on Saturday night?"

"I didn't say that. Look, Miss Allan, that's got nothing to do with it."

"It's got everything to do with it, Off-i-cer. All my life it's had everything to do with it. My Mama's worked for Jack Lynes's mother since she was sixteen, and when she was twenty-two one of their high-toned friends came to her room in the middle of the night and there wasn't a thing she could do about it. She lived in their house and she worked in their kitchen, and she couldn't tell them what had happened later on when she found she was pregnant. Mrs. Lynes gave her hell for leading a loose life and Mr. Lynes said it was what you could expect from a nigger gal. Okay, Officer?"

"No. It's not okay."

"You know what they used to say. A Southern boy hasn't grown up until he's had a nigger gal. You ever had a nigger gal, Officer Bealle?"

"Cut that out! You don't have to—" His face was burning.

"Don't have to what?"

"Talk like that."

"It embarrasses you, Officer Bealle?"

He stabbed his notebook with his pencil. "You don't have to run yourself down like that."

"You didn't answer my question."

"I told you you don't have to talk like that."

"That wasn't the question. The one before that. Well, have you?"

Angus put his notebook in his pocket and stood up. "I've got a lot to do. I'd best be going."

"You think what they all think. Black people are all like that."

"You shut up about that; you don't know what I think!"

"But you tell jokes about it. Well, I'll tell you something, Mr. White Police Officer. I've been to three shrinks because of what Mark Nailles did to me and what one of them did to Mama. One of them said what I needed was a white man who could really do it, and he was just the fellow. You're looking at one frigid gal, Officer, who's never been able to really get it off with anybody, black or white. You think I couldn't kill Mark Nailles? I could kill him and cut him up in little pieces for what he did to me." She was crying. She turned her back to Angus and put her hands over her face.

Angus picked up a dish towel and walked around to face her, reached out, and touched her arm. She took one hand away, saw the towel, and took it from him. He waited while she caught her breath, wiped her eyes on the towel, and blew into it.

"I never thought about you or any woman that way."

She reached out and put a hand on his arm. Angus looked down at it, let it stay there. "You must think I'm one big bag of rottenness."

"I told you you don't know what I think." He put his hand over hers and left it there until she moved away.

"You want to know about Mark Nailles and me, right?" She was all business, her voice contained. "I came on pretty strong there, didn't I?" Angus nodded. "Sorry. It's just that I get so goddamn mad when—"

"It's okay."

"Mama knows I know who my father is. She never told me but she knows I know. If it turns out you have to know I'll tell you, but I don't think it will. I guess I was lucky. The Lyneses paid to send me away to school after what happened with Mark Nailles. From school I went to Smith College. I didn't get pregnant, and that was a great relief to everybody including me. But I'll tell you this. If it had been one of their daughters it wouldn't have ended any differently. They'd have hushed it all up and everything would go along just as it always has." She put out her hand, looking steadily at Angus. He took it, shook it briefly, and let go. "I'll be here until Monday. You seem like one of the good guys. Next time it won't be in the white folks' kitchen, so maybe I won't mouth off like I did."

"I may want to ask you some more questions."

"I'll tell you something. I hated Mark Nailles but I didn't kill him."

"Nobody said you did."

"You think I might have."

"I don't think anything yet."

Angus picked up his hat and went out the kitchen door. From the terrace behind the hedge he heard the talk and laughter from the luncheon table. He wondered which of the women there might be Serene's sister-in-law and if she knew. Nothing about their voices told him that they cared what had happened to Mark Nailles the night before.

CHAPTER 11

Angus sat in his car but did not start it. The anger and venom in Serene's voice was something new to him. She was right; he had heard the jokes, listened to the talk, even wondered what it would be like. But it wasn't just black; he wondered what it would be like with a lot of white girls, too. There were things he'd like to talk with Serene about. But no way could he talk to her about that.

He was about to drive off when Pat Rillbon came around the house in his pickup truck and parked beside the garage. He wore a khaki shirt and trousers and heavy work shoes. He was a thin, wiry man, his skin weathered by his time in the open air, his heavy hair still thick around his temples. Most of it was covered with a green cloth cap with a John Deere logo on it. His lean face heralded the lean good looks of his son, Jeff, but age had taken away the freshness and left the hardness. His blue green eyes looked straight at Angus without guile.

He lifted a bushel basket from the truck and carried it toward the kitchen door. As Rillbon stopped beside the patrol car Angus saw heaps of green lettuce, bunches of asparagus and radishes, and a smaller basket under the lettuces filled with green peas.

"Kind of early for asparagus, isn't it, Mr. Rillbon?" Angus wasn't sure if that were so, but he wanted to give Serene a few moments before encountering anyone.

"Is, but it's coming along. These are the first peas." He put the basket down. "I'm glad I caught you, Angus. Something I have to say."

"I was going to hunt you up, Mr. Rillbon."

"I told the sheriff everything I know about this business this morning." He leaned forward with both hands against the door of Angus's car. Angus saw the halo of white skin at the edges of his wide wedding band. Despite the toughness of his hands his nails were scrubbed clean.

"What I wanted to talk to you about was Peaches."

"What about her?"

"She told me she found a hatchet that was used to kill Nailles."

"She showed me the hatchet but I don't know about the rest of it."

"Will you show it to me?"

"Why do you want to see it?"

"If it was one of ours, I could identify it."

"Are you missing a hatchet?"

"I haven't checked. I'd know if I could see it."

Angus pushed the door open as Rillbon stepped back and picked up his basket. They walked to the trunk; Angus took out the plastic bag, opened it, and held it out. The weight of the hatchet stretched the thin plastic so that it was difficult to see, and Angus rolled the bag up in his hands until the hatchet was in plain view.

The cutting edge and part of the blade were encrusted with dark blood; some of it had spattered on the handle where it entered the steel head.

Rillbon squinted his blue eyes, peering at the weapon. "You want to turn it over, Angus?"

Angus held the handle through the plastic and flipped the hatchet over. There was less blood on that side.

"That's a chicken feather there, stuck in the head. It's one of my tools, Angus. Somebody used it to kill a rooster after a fight. You'll find that's chicken blood on there."

"It'll have to be tested."

"Sure. But it will test out chicken blood."

Angus wrapped the bag around the hatchet and returned it to the trunk. "Did Peaches tell you how she happened to find it?"

Rillbon waited a long minute before he answered. "She said she was back there this morning, looking for wild daisies. They grow along the fence there."

"It's early for wild daisies, Mr. Rillbon."

"She tell you something different, Angus?" Rillbon's voice was hoarse and he cleared his throat to remove whatever emotion was stopping it. When Angus did not answer, he went on. "Look here, Angus, don't get some idea that she had anything to do with this killing. She never even heard of the man before this morning."

"Did Peaches tell you that?"

Rillbon looked at the ground, ran a hand nervously over his chin and mouth. "That business this morning with Mrs. Cumberley. I don't know what she meant, jumping on Peaches like that. Peaches shouldn't have done what she did. I guess you know we've had some problems with her, Angus. But she swears she never saw him before."

Angus was sorry for Rillbon, if he believed Peaches's lie. "What about you? Did you see Nailles last night?"

"He was moving around a lot. He came with that crowd from Charlottesville and sat with them for a while. But I wasn't really watching him. Never occurred to me somebody was going to kill him."

"I need the names of those people."

"There was a lawyer named Hamphall, they call him Shakey, I don't know his full name. And a fellow from a bank named Billy Bartoe. I don't know if the woman with him was his wife. The other woman was Mrs. Chesmire, lives over near Yancey's Mill. She's got a cockpit at her place. Never heard she has a husband. There were a couple of men I didn't know. Somebody said one of them was a judge."

"Did you see them leave?"

"They were gone before the fights were over. That's all I know."

Angus felt that Rillbon was trying to avoid talking about Nailles more than he had to. He probably knew that Peaches was lying about knowing him. "When was the last time you saw Nailles?"

Rillbon shrugged. "I couldn't really say, Angus. Like I said, he was moving around a lot. Went outside the barn a time or two, I think, or to the toilet. He was there all night."

"There's a toilet in the barn?"

"Mr. Fess Lynes put it in when he fixed up the barn. It's next to the room that's used as an office. There were a lot of people using it last night."

"What about the others; did they move around, too?"

"Jack Lynes's friends? I suppose they did. I was in and out."

"What about Jeff? Was he there last night?"

Rillbon's voice rose sharply. "Now look here, you leave Jeff out of this. He was over in Charlottesville last night. He came on Nailles's body this morning, but that's all. His name's going to be in all the papers because he found the body, but that's all; none of the rest of my family is going to get involved in it. When you find out that's chicken blood on that hatchet, you can just keep Peaches out of it." He turned abruptly and picked up his basket, walking rapidly away toward the kitchen steps. Angus watched him, angry with himself at his clumsiness in questioning Rillbon. He was not telling him everything he knew about Nailles's movements.

He reached for his radio. Ethel Sue Shufflet told him the sheriff wasn't available. "He's gone home and he doesn't want to be disturbed. He's flat of his back and says he can't get up to answer the telephone or the radio."

"What if I went out there to see him?"

"I wouldn't if I was you. You know how he gets when he hurts."

"I've got to talk to somebody."

"Wait a minute." There was silence until she called back. "What about Mr. Cumberley? I see his car in the parking lot. He's in his office."

"Maybe I can talk to him. Thanks."

While he was talking Serene came out of the kitchen and walked across to the garage. He watched the loose white dress she wore swing against her long legs. She did not look his way. The question she had asked him flashed across his mind as he remembered the touch of her hand on his arm. He shifted inside his clothes and drew a quick breath through his mouth. Then he put his car in gear and drove down the lane to the highway.

CHAPTER 12

Phoebeville on Saturday afternoon was deserted. Bushannans who had business at the courthouse took care of it during the week; those who had money to spend took it to Charlottesville and Richmond. The Farmers Co-op stayed open until noon. One man was pumping gasoline at Buck Bolton's Exxon station; there were two cars parked in front of the pharmacy and four in the parking lot next to the Super-Buy Supermarket. Hatchett's Chrysler-Plymouth had gone out of business the winter before and stood empty, the plastic flags over the empty lot moving idly in the small breeze. The old redbrick courthouse was cool and deserted under the new shade of the maples and elms.

Angus pulled up behind the sheriff's department building. Ethel Sue was painting lacquer on her nails; she looked up and went back to her brush. She could not read, write, or paint her nails with her mouth closed; her jaw hung open in the agony of concentration.

"I didn't get any subpoenas served today," Angus announced. "And it's almost time for Vern to relieve me."

"You going to tell me about it? The murder, I mean?" Ethel Sue did not look up as she brushed the rosy lacquer over her long nails. "I been waiting here all day to hear about it. The sheriff wouldn't tell me anything." Her lips opened wider as she drew the brush along her talons.

Angus looked down at what she was doing. "How'd you get your fingernails to be long like that? You bite your nails."

She waved a hand in the air, fingers spread. "You get them at the Peoples in Charlottesville. You stick them on over your real nails." She looked up at him from under the fringe of tightly curled blond hair and brushed it aside with the back of her hand. "You're trying to change the subject on me. What about the murder?"

"A man named Mark Nailles was killed some time last night. Somebody cut him up really bad."

"You know who did it yet?"

"Could have been anybody. Those people out there, they act like nothing's happened at all. All the women are sitting around having lunch and talking like nothing has happened, all the men went off to play golf."

"Was there lots of hollering and screaming when they found the body and all?"

"If there was, I wasn't there. The sheriff sent me off to find the dead man's son."

Ethel Sue waved her hands in the air, blowing on them as they passed in front of her face.

"He's supposed to be out at Sweet Valley," Angus said.

"You mean it's that Nailles?"

"What do you mean, that Nailles?"

"I mean Brod Nailles, he's one of them. I've seen him around town lots of times. He comes in on the truck every few days."

"You know him?"

"Not know him, really. I've talked to him a time or two, that's all. He's kind of weird. I mean, he's kind of cute-looking, but hard to talk to. You know? When we were in Charlottesville last winter at the basketball tournament, somebody showed me a man she said was his father. Can you believe it? Now he's been murdered right here in Bushanna County."

"Who was it who showed him to you?"

"It was Peaches. She knew who he was, she said he'd been out there at Copperfields. She told me he was Brod Nailles's father." She held her hands out. "You like this color? I don't know if I can take it off without ruining these nails. What do you think?"

"Looks okay to me. You mean Peaches knows Brod Nailles?"

"Oh, she hasn't dated him or like that. But there aren't that many cute boys around; you get to know who they are, Angus. He didn't have a lot of interest in Peaches, you want to know the truth." There was satisfaction in her tone.

"When was the last time you saw Brod Nailles?"

"Last week, I think. He was in the Co-op when I went by there to talk to Lucille Murdock. She had her hair fixed in Richmond when she was there, she wanted me to see it. This man in Richmond cut it in sort of a cap—" She used her hands to demonstrate. "—so I went by. He was there. He's really neat."

"You said he was weird."

"Maybe not weird. Just hard to get to know."

"But he's already got a girl, Ethel Sue."

"Her? She's been out there since that place started. She's old. She must be thirty-*five.*"

"Women thirty-five can be very attractive. Even older than that."

"Yes, but she's ugly. And she can be hateful sometimes. She doesn't even wear makeup. Who do you know that's thirty-five you think is so attractive?"

"Nobody in particular. I just said that."

"Then why are you blushing?"

The door behind him opened and Angus turned to hide his confusion. It was Vern Wishburn, the deputy on the next shift. He was in his forties, his uniform too small for the twenty pounds he had gained since he bought it. Vern had been on the force for fifteen years. He had a mean streak that made people wary of him. The meanness showed in his eyes, dark peepholes in the puffiness of his face, and in his mouth, set in a perpetual sneer. His wife ran a beauty shop in their house. Everybody in Phoebeville except Vern knew that she was shacking up with the druggist. He went there to get his hair cut twice a month while Vern was on duty. He had been going there for six years and she had made no appointments afterward for five.

Vern got very little information from Angus about the murder, which made him surlier than usual, and when Angus told him that he had not had a chance to serve the subpoenas Vern said he'd be goddamned if he was going to do Angus's work for him. He left the office and drove off throwing gravel.

When Ethel Sue left, the rescue squad took over the radio for the weekend. Angus stayed on writing up his reports. When he finished, he began trying to construct a timetable of the night before. There were lots of blanks between nine when the fights started and the next morning when Jeff found Nailles's body.

He knew that the sheriff had a telephone by his bed, so he took a chance and dialed him. Rowe answered, his voice guttural.

"It's Angus, Sheriff."

"What the hell you want, Bealle? Didn't Ethel Sue tell you I don't want no calls?"

"It's about the Nailles case, Sheriff."

"Can't Wishburn handle it? Ain't he on duty tonight?"

"He's got his own rounds to make."

"Then what the hell is it?"

"Are you authorizing overtime on this case?"

"Overtime? On Saturday night? What the hell for?"

"There's a lot of people to be tracked down, Sheriff."

"You go on home; you can get at it again tomorrow. Can't have a lot of deputies over there messing up the Lynes's weekend. Wasn't their fault the fellow got killed. If there's going to be overtime, Skinker ought to get it. He ain't had but a couple of hours when that tank truck overturned."

CHAPTER 13

Angus found Cap Cumberley at his desk in the inner room. He was in his shirt sleeves. The circles under his eyes made him look older than Angus knew he was. The desk in front of him was stacked with law books and papers. Angus stood before him, looking down at the jumble; he wondered how Cumberley could make sense of the mess before him. The late afternoon was still, no air blowing through the open windows.

"You got some time to talk, Mr. Cumberley?"

"That's all I have, Angus. Time to talk." Cumberley shifted the papers on his desk about, putting a law book over the sheaf of papers he had been reading. Angus saw from the exposed corner that it was photocopied from a book or magazine.

"Don't want to interrupt."

"Nothing here to interrupt. I'm here because I've got nowhere else to go." He rubbed his eyes with the back of his hand, then looked at his hand while he picked at the adhesive bandage on his palm. He looked tired and older than usual.

Angus pulled up a worn Windsor chair. "There's some things I don't know about, I thought you might help me."

"If I can, Angus."

"It's about the Nailles murder. What I don't understand is how people like that can do like they do. Here somebody they know has been killed in their own house, you might say, and Mr. Lynes and the other men go off and play golf. Their wives—the ladies there—sit around and laugh like nothing's happened."

"Life goes on, Angus. Mark Nailles wasn't worth crying over; they all know that."

"They all say that, but still they ought to care some."

"People have only so much caring in the bank, Angus. We can't spend it on people not worth caring about. A lot of us are already overdrawn. You look at them. Jack Lynes and his wife. Who else is there?"

Angus took out his notebook and flipped it open. "There's a Mr. Foster Glove and his wife. Her name's—"

"Tottsy."

"Sir?"

"Her name's Charlotte. They call her Tottsy."

"Yes, sir. And a Mr. and Mrs. B-a-r-r-e-l-l. They call it Barl."

"Sally Carter and Biston. Bitsy. She's Nailles's sister."

"That's what I was told. You'd think she'd care some, but it doesn't look like she does, one bit."

"She'll live through it. Biston's not much, but he's got a name to go with her money. Her brother made a lot of money for both of them in real estate. What about Nick Mathers? He there?"

"He came this morning. He told everybody he had car trouble but he was lying."

"If they gave out Olympic medals for playing the field Nick would win the gold and Fossy Glove the silver. The only trouble his car has is that it gets parked in the wrong driveways."

"Yes, sir. He said he stayed the night at the motel at Bunts Crossroads, but that's been closed since March. He was in Richmond all night. With Mrs. Nailles."

Cumberley looked up, startled. "He told you that?"

"Yes, sir. He's been seeing her for a year or so, he said. He's not much of a man. I mean, lying like that, and everything."

"Not much, I suppose. None of them—us—is, really. Does Mrs. Mathers know about Nick and Nailles's wife?"

"He said he was going to tell her when I left him. But I guess she already knows."

"This kind of thing will hurt. She's a cut above the rest. Who else is there?"

Angus was silent. Cumberley looked at him, pushed a book aside, pulled it back. "It's okay, Angus. I know who else."

"Mrs. Cumberley."

"I'm out of that now. Who's there with her? Billy Parsons? Freddie Hashbourne? Hank McFerlin?"

"No, sir. It wasn't any of them. That's all that are there."

"No partner for the odd lady? Kenyon Lynes wouldn't like that. It makes her table unbalanced."

"Yes, sir."

"There must be somebody for the lady."

"Yes, sir. Seems she's been—she—" Angus looked at the floor, trying to get the words out.

"You're trying to tell me she's been seeing Mark Nailles?"

"Yes, sir. That's what I'm told."

"He wasn't staying at Copperfields, was he?"

"No, sir. Mrs. Lynes said he wasn't welcome there."

"I didn't think he was." Cumberley rubbed his hand across his face. "She was bound to get to him sooner or later. There aren't many left."

"The way you talk, sir, all they want to do is—" Angus made a helpless gesture with his hands.

"That's all they have to do. Not a one of them has to think five minutes about where the money comes from. Except maybe Fossy Glove. Jack Lynes's great-grandfather made a fortune stealing land from soldiers coming home from the Confederate war. He started a bank. His grandfather put his money in mines and railroads and his father put his in chemicals. Jack's loaded. Tottsy Glove's father had a paper mill he ran into something big during World War II. Lois Mathers inherited some land that's now covered with shopping centers. The same with Nailles and Sally Carter. They've made a hell of a lot of money from it. Foster Glove's a broker; he hasn't got any real money. Capital, that is. You can bet Tottsy doesn't let him get his hands on hers."

"What about Barrell?"

"Biston Barrell. He's got enough to get by. If somebody killed him, the ground would run blue with his blood. He's kin to everybody south of the Potomac one way or another. That's why Sally Carter married him. Christ knows it wasn't for his brains or for his manly beauty."

Angus grinned. "The sheriff said he was a fruity-faced little man."

"The sheriff is unkind. Observant, but unkind."

"What about the other one, Mathers?"

"Lois has more money than he does, but he does okay. He knows how to make money. Pulls in a lot from the law firm his old man started. Mathers McFerlin Cullip and Gee." Cumberley's face sagged; he ran a hand over his mouth. "I started out with that firm. Amy grew up with that crowd. They all went to the same schools, the same dancing classes. They're so ingrown they even have a special way of dancing."

"You think any of them could have killed Mark Nailles?"

"Any one of them could, Angus. The question is which one of them did."

"The sheriff's dead set it's Nailles's son. Because we can't find him. He's been living out at Sweet Valley for six months or so. He went away somewhere last Thursday."

"Did you check with his mother?"

"Mrs. Lynes asked one of her friends to tell her what had happened. That's how Mathers found out; he was there. They told me out at Sweet Valley the son's been living with one of the women out there. She's older than he is."

"You talk to her?"

"Not yet. She's in Charlottesville. She's in med school, but she lives at Sweet Valley. And there's somebody else. Mrs. Lynes's cook has her daughter visiting there. We'll have to look into her, too."

"Why do you think she might be involved?"

"Her name's Serene." Angus picked his hat up from his lap, ran his finger around the brim. "She—she told me that this Nailles raped her once, when she was sixteen."

Cumberley's mouth opened and he swallowed twice before he spoke. "She told you that?"

"You should have heard her, Mr. Cumberley. Can you believe a man doing something like that to a sixteen-year-old girl?"

"I can believe it of Mark Nailles. Yes."

"He was already married at the time. She said one of Mr. Lynes's father's friends practically did the same thing to her mother."

"Good God in Heaven! Did she say who it was?"

"No, sir. But she said it made her mother pregnant. With her. She said she's the sister of one of the men there. That means Mather, or Barrell or Glove."

Cumberley picked up a pencil and drew circles on a yellow legal pad, one inside another, until he got to the center of the page. He stabbed the bull's-eye with his pencil and threw it down. He stared at the yellow target while tears formed in his eyes and ran down his cheeks. His mouth was open but he did not sob. He pulled the sheaf of paper from under the law book, balled it up in his hands, spun around in his chair, and tossed it at the empty fireplace. He put his face in his hands, ran the tips of his fingers under his eyes, then took a handkerchief from his pocket and blew his nose. His voice when he finally spoke was spongy.

"Somebody did the world a favor last night, Angus. When you catch whoever did it, don't expect me to prosecute."

"Sorry, Mr. Cumberley. I didn't mean to say anything that would upset you. I don't even know what it was I said."

Cumberley put his handkerchief away, got up, and looked out the window at the shady lawn. He took a deep breath, put an arm out, and leaned against the windowsill. "My daughter would be twenty years old this summer. She died last year. That's all, Angus. That's all." He turned around. "No. That's not all. When she died, she was pregnant. Her mother and I didn't know it until after she died. No way I could know. We were divorced, and Emily lived with her mother until she moved out two years ago.

"She was a lovely girl, bright and pretty. Nobody knew she was having—was seeing somebody. She didn't want to go to college right away after she finished school. I suppose she got lost in the shuffle between me and Amy. She got a job as a waitress and moved into a place of her own. I didn't like it but young women are different now. When I was her age, if they got jobs at all it was some nice place like a decorator's shop or a law office through a friend of their parents. Or they went to New York and worked for a magazine. Mostly they went to college and got married and spent their lives volunteering with the Junior League or the Museum. We didn't even know who the man was she was seeing."

Angus did not break the silence when Cumberley stopped. After a long moment he went on. "She was three months pregnant and hadn't told anybody. There was an autopsy and the doctors said she probably died after trying to abort. Do you know what they do at an autopsy, Angus? Have you ever seen an autopsy? I haven't, but I know what they do. That lovely girl!

You know what they said they found? They found out she was pregnant, but she died from an air embolism."

"I don't know what that is."

"It's air in the vascular system. In the veins. That's what made them think she must have died from attempting an abortion. She didn't go to a clinic like so many women do today."

"I'm sorry about your daughter, Mr. Cumberley. I understand how you must feel."

"There's no way you can understand how I feel, Angus. Mark Nailles was just one more of a crowd out there who don't give a damn how much trouble they cause. The man my daughter was seeing didn't have the common decency to show himself after she died. Nobody in the apartment house where she lived knew who he was, nobody came to us and said he was sorry she was dead. She was going to have his baby, for God's sake!" Cumberley pounded the windowsill hard with his fist, once, took a deep breath, and returned to his desk. He sat down and began to shuffle papers. "You ought to get the state police in on this, you know."

"The sheriff won't do it. You get them in, he says, you lose control of everything. He's made up his mind it's Nailles's son, all he wants is for me to find him. Mr. Cumberley, isn't there something can be done about the sheriff?"

"He's an elected constitutional officer. He can get beat in an election."

"Nobody's running against him."

"You can raise the question of malfeasance or misfeasance and get a grand jury on it. You want to do that?"

"I don't even know what it means. I just want to see things done right."

"Then you ought to charge him with misfeasance: Doing things in an improper manner, or misusing his power."

"No, sir. I don't want to do that."

"The people of the county elected him, it's up to the people to get rid of him. In the meantime, Angus, you just try to do the best you can."

"I can't do it all, Mr. Cumberley. We've got six men including the sheriff, not even two on a shift. Only one sometimes. Most days we serve warrants and garnishments, the rest of the time we spend checking out boys riding dirt bikes on people's lanes or somebody's dog bothering people. There was a burglary last week at the Exxon station, but we caught them right away. This is the first real murder we've ever had that I can remember."

"You'd like to be sheriff someday, Angus?"

"Yes, sir. But not like Sheriff Rowe."

"You do the best you can. You'll make it."

"It looks like nobody cares if we get the man who killed Nailles. Serene—Miss Allan—said he belonged in the White House, not the Jail House. Somebody ought to care."

"As long as you care, that's enough."

"With the sheriff laid up nothing much is getting done. Everything is getting cold. Maybe that's the way he wants it. But even if he's somebody who's better dead, that's not the way to do it. I'm a policeman and so is the sheriff. We've got to find out who did it no matter who it hurts. The sheriff has to work for a living, but he's just like them. All he's got on his mind is—you know. Getting it off with some woman."

"What else do you have on your mind, Angus?" Cumberley smiled.

Angus felt his face getting hot. He knew Cumberley was ribbing him good-naturedly. "I don't think about it all the time. And I don't try to do it all the time."

"Even if you'd like to?"

Angus grinned. "No point in thinking about it when you're not much good at it."

"It can tear you up, Angus. Take it from somebody who's been through it. It destroyed my marriage and killed my daughter. Now maybe it's killed Mark Nailles. But you're young. You forget what I've been saying. It's Saturday evening. You go out tonight and be young. You've got a girl?"

"Not really. There's somebody out at Sweet Valley I'd kind of like to get to know better, but she says she's not interested in that sort of thing."

"You go out there and make her interested. You're young and healthy. But watch out and don't let it eat you up. Forget about all this and have a good time. It will all work out. It usually does."

CHAPTER 14

A heavy beat was coming from the shed when Angus drove up. The sides were open to the night, spilling the flashing colored lights that pulsed with the music into the dark. A dozen couples, not all of opposing sexes, danced in the middle of the floor. The faint smell of marijuana and body heat blew across his face as he walked in. He knew that grass was tolerated, but there was no problem with heavy stuff. Nobody did any dealing in anything.

The girl called Hebe was dancing with a seven-year-old Angus knew was Annabel's daughter. Hebe was in faded jeans and a kind of shawl made of sheer material tie-dyed in shades of lavender and blue. She wore nothing under the shawl; her generous breasts bobbed with the rhythm, the dark aureoles of her nipples veiled by the fabric but showing though. The child was awkward, tall for her age, with straight blonde hair down to her shoulders. It was the first time Angus had ever seen her smiling. Two men in their twenties, whom Moon had told him were lovers, danced together near Hebe and the child. Vee and Rebo were in the band, Vee on guitar and Rebo playing an electric organ. The beat was loud and heavy, but Angus was not impressed with its quality.

He did not see Moon among the dancers or with the people standing around drinking beer. Nothing stronger than beer was permitted at Sweet Valley, and that only on weekends and special occasions.

He found Annabel standing by herself with a glass of something, not beer, in her hand. She was a tall woman, thin and awkward, with a long face and heavy chin. Her black hair, showing some gray at the sides, was cut short, but not mannishly. She wore a man's shirt and short cotton skirt in a bright print pattern. She was not good-looking but a brightness in her face and a look of interest in her eyes dispelled the first impression of plainness.

The spectators greeted Angus with a wave or a nod; a girl in a hand-crocheted open-work dress through which Angus could see her nakedness underneath examined him openly and frankly. A man standing beside her did the same. He looked quickly away from them and went up to Annabel.

She put the contents of her glass down with a gulp and set the glass on a counter. "Vee told me about Brod's old man," she said. "We rapped about it this afternoon to get our feelings about violence out. We decided it wasn't a problem here. Brod's gone, you know."

"I know. I've got to find him."

"Don't come to me about it. He left, but he didn't say where he was going."

"You can't make a guess?"

"It's not my business. He's trying to work out his hostilities. It's those upper-class values he's got."

"Vee said you and he were—you know—good friends."

"If you mean we were sleeping together, that's right. If you mean we had some kind of real relationship, forget it. He had a lot of problems, and I was one of them. I just don't want to be his mother."

"He didn't give you any idea where he went?"

"He didn't give me anything. He left some shirts and a pair of socks. His dirty laundry. He didn't leave anything of himself here."

Angus looked around. The girl in the crocheted dress had moved so that she stood close behind him. She smiled at him. Angus said to Annabel, "Can we go somewhere else, where we can talk? I want to know about Brod Nailles."

"You want to, we can go to my room."

"Isn't there somewhere else?"

"You think you'll lose your virtue there?"

"I didn't mean it that way."

"Neither did I. If you want it that way, all you have to do is turn around."

She led him around the room full of dancers out into the open and across the grassy compound to her dormitory. It was a neat two-story building with a sloping roof, open stairways, and a gallery that ran along the second floor. A dozen rooms opened off the gallery; Angus knew that everyone at Sweet Valley had a single room if they chose. Married couples and unmarried pairs shared larger quarters.

Annabel's room, with walls of unpainted pine, was neat and orderly. There was a double bed with some batik pillows she had made, a macramé wall hanging that struck Angus as being singularly unattractive, two posters, a chest of drawers, and an open clothes rack on which hung half a dozen garments. Two bookshelves held medical textbooks and paperbacks, and a work table was piled with more books. The high ceiling and clerestory windows at the peak of the sloping roof made the room cool and breezy. A screen door left it open to the gallery.

"Some of the others here say I wasn't supportive enough of Brod," Annabel said as they walked in. "I said it's one thing to be supportive and another to be a mother. I don't like being a mother. Never did."

"But don't you have a child?"

"That doesn't mean I like being a mother. I had her because I wanted to have a child. I didn't have her because I wanted to be a mother. They let me have Trade at a time when I really wanted to have a baby. Now we all look after her with the rest of the children."

"What about her father? Is he still here?"

"He split soon after she was born."

"What did you mean, they let you have her?"

"We decided a long time ago it wasn't going to work here if everybody got pregnant any time they wanted to. It's one of the rules. The committee decides if you can have a baby if you want one." She laughed. "I see what you're thinking. How the hell can a committee keep you from getting pregnant? Of course sometimes one comes along without permission. Everybody accepts that. Okay? But this place wouldn't have worked if we had all those babies to look after. I've been here for thirteen years, ever since I was twenty-two. We had some rough going getting started. We had to have rules. That was one of Brod's problems; he didn't like all the rules."

"He didn't get along here?"

"Nobody gets along all the time. Brod didn't get along more than most. We've got over sixty people here; some get along, some don't. The ones that don't mostly move on. Somebody comes along to take their places. Hey, man. This is a commune. Everybody works, everybody shares. Everybody's equal, everybody has to fit in."

"Brod didn't fit in?"

"He wasn't ready to get rid of his bourgeois ideas. It's not his fault. A lot of them who come here can't."

"Is that why he left?"

"He had his reasons. They come here with a lot of ideas about what Sweet Valley's all about. They think it's some kind of utopia. Everything's going to feel good just because they're here. Or they come to get out of the way of something, or to hide from something. I don't mean crime or like that, but like middle-class parents or some materialistic job."

"But everybody here has a job."

"Nobody gets a free ride. We take turns working in the garden, working in the shops, kitchen detail, everything. We change the committees so nobody gets to think he's bigger than anybody else. And we can outvote the committee anytime we don't think they're right."

"What about you? You go to med school."

"I do my share. The committee decided I could go. They're paying for it, so they have a say in what I do."

"Are you going to stay here when you finish?"

"That scares me sometimes, thinking about it. I've been here so long. Somebody's got to break the hold the capitalistic doctors have on the health of the country."

"About Brod. Did he tell you about the fight he had with his father?"

"He spent most of his time fighting with his father, according to him."

"This was a real fight, in his office. He broke his father's jaw."

"Sure. He told me. His old man was trying to move in on him, on his girlfriend. Brod found out and went to his office and beat up on him."

"Do you know who the girl was?"

She waited a moment and Angus had a feeling she wasn't

going to tell him all she knew. "He told me, but names don't mean anything here. We use the names we want to. Brod said his old man was queer on young girls. Not little girls. Young women. Typical male bourgeois attitude. He got her pregnant and she died."

Angus felt his heart grab; he had trouble swallowing. "Where did this happen?" His voice was hoarse.

"Richmond, I suppose. That's where they all live. It was a rotten thing to happen, but that's what you get when you live in a rotten society like that."

"How long has Brod been here?"

Annabel shrugged. "Six, eight months. It's a good thing he's gone, you know. The committee wouldn't let him stay here when his probation is up."

"Do you know why she died?"

"Brod said it was in the papers that it was from complications of pregnancy; probably a botched abortion. People like that try to cover up for each other."

"Do you know what an embolism is?"

She turned her head quickly, looking at him and then looking away. "Jesus! You shift gears in a hurry. It's an obstruction in the blood vessels. Something carried in the blood vessels that obstructs the flow of blood."

"Can being pregnant cause it?"

"You don't get pregnant in the blood vessels, Buster. Being pregnant causes lots of things including grief and pain. When Brod showed up here he was looking for a cradle. He wanted to be safe and warm. He picked me out because I was older, he thought I could be his mother substitute. I let him work that through because he had something else I wanted."

"What's that?"

"An honest-to-God roll in the hay." She said it matter-of-factly but her body moved in a way that made Angus uncomfortable. "Like you. You've got that look." She studied him from under her short bangs.

"Now come on. You don't have to—"

"Talk that way? I didn't say I wanted you to; I said you've got the same look Brod has. That doesn't mean you can do anything. The first time we tried he couldn't do a thing. I had to make him realize I wasn't his mother. After that, my God!" She waved her hands in a hallelujah.

"You say it like you're trying to get a rise out of somebody."

"It's no secret. He was a stud and that's what I wanted."

"But you don't know where he went?"

"Or when he will come back. We don't make them stay here. They're free to go."

"Not to go out and kill their fathers."

"They're free to go for whatever the reasons. You think Brod killed his old man?"

"The sheriff does. He wants to find him so he can wrap everything up."

"I'm sorry I can't help you."

"If you hear from him will you let me know?"

"So you can arrest him?"

"So I can talk to him."

She looked hard at him for a moment without speaking. "Do you like being a cop?"

"Sure. I like it fine. It's what I want to do."

"Beating people up, imposing your will on others, trampling on the rights of citizens?"

"Oh come on! It's not like that."

"Carrying a big stick like you're a stud all the time?"

"I don't carry a stick. What makes you talk like that?"

"You ever hear of penis envy? You think I've got it, right?"

"I don't even know what you're talking about."

She laughed. It wasn't a merry sound, just dry and mirthless. "I don't think you do. So okay. You're just doing your job. If I hear from Brod I'll let you know. Okay?"

"Okay."

"But you've got to promise me you won't railroad him."

"We don't do that. I'll do whatever I have to do. Understand that."

"Okay." She stood up. "I said you had that look about you. Would you like to try it with me?"

She was not trying to be seductive. She stood straight and looked straight at him. Angus shook his head. Getting in bed with Annabel was the last thing he wanted to do then. "I've got some things to do—I mean—It's not that I—"

"Okay. I don't turn you on. You can say it. It won't be the first time I've heard that."

"I didn't mean it that way."

"But it ends up the same way, doesn't it?" She went to the door and opened it. It took Angus a moment to realize that the music at the dance had stopped. The lights were on and he could see people moving about in the shed.

He walked with Annabel across the common. At the wide doors Vee called out to him. "Hey, man. We been looking for you. Come see who's here." He waved toward a clutch of people in a corner. The crowd separated as they walked across the room. Angus saw a young man standing with a can of beer in his hand, looking toward them.

"For Jesus' sake!" he heard Annabel say. "Brod's back!"

CHAPTER 15

Brod Nailles was a short man, not more than five eight, with broad muscular shoulders showing through his dirty T-shirt. His full blond hair framed his dark eyes and full lips and set off his darker beard. He stood waiting for Angus to come to him.

"You know about your father?" Angus asked. Brod nodded. "You know we—the police have been looking for you?"

A wave of the beer can said "I heard," or "So what?"

"He's a policeman, Brod," Annabel said from behind Angus.

"It doesn't matter," Brod Nailles said. His voice was soft.

"I'm not on duty."

"But that doesn't count, does it?"

"No. I suppose it doesn't count. I came out here this morning to tell you what had happened to your father. Now I'd like to ask you some questions."

"You can use my place," Annabel said.

"This isn't going to mean trouble is it, Angus?" Vee's voice was anxious. "For the commune, I mean?"

"No. I just want to talk to Brod."

"We keep things on the level here, you know that."

"I know that, Vee. This doesn't have anything to do with Sweet Valley."

"Except that they're harboring a fugitive," Brod's voice was low.

"It's not that way, Brod," Annabel said. "But you watch out, anyway."

"I'm not here to arrest anybody," Angus told the crowd. "But I do have to talk to Brod. If I do it now I won't have to do it later with my uniform on."

"There's an office over there," Vee said. "You can use it."

Brod handed his can of beer to Vee and walked ahead of Angus toward the door. The crowd had moved away but watched the two men as Angus closed the door of the office behind him.

"I heard he was cut up something bad," Brod said. "You know who did it yet?"

"We're still investigating."

"I didn't kill him, if that's what you are asking."

"If you tell me where you've been we can settle that right now."

"Suppose I don't tell you?"

"Then I'll have to find out some other way. Either way we've got to know. They said you left here sometime Thursday; nobody knew where you had gone."

"I didn't tell anybody where I was going."

"That's why I've got to ask. Your mother hasn't heard from you."

"You leave my mother out of this!"

"Annabel didn't know either."

"Annabel doesn't care. All she does is make trouble."

"She's not making trouble for you now."

"Well who does care where I am or what I do?"

"You could say I do."

"Only because you're a cop who's trying to pin some murder on me."

"Only if you did it. When was the last time you saw him—your father?"

"I don't remember."

"Have you seen him since you had that fight with him?"

"Who told you about that?"

"Was that the last time?"

"You know so much, you tell me."

"I'm asking you, Brod. Look, I'm trying to get to the bottom of this. I told you, if you didn't do it, there'll be no sweat."

"No sweat for you. Sweat for me, though, man. You think just because I didn't beat him to death, nobody's going to tie me to him? You're crazy, man. Everywhere I go they tie me to him. My mother does; all her friends do. He's got a reputation reaches all the way to Philadelphia, man. Likes them young, Mark Nailles does. You're just like your father, boy. That's what my mother said. Just like him. Did you know that she was pregnant with me when they got married? That's why they got married. You didn't know that, did you, Sheriff?"

"I'm not the sheriff. Yes, I knew that."

"See? Even out here in the boondocks they heard that."

"I was told that today, Brod."

"It would not have made any difference to her if she had liked him. She can't stand the sight of him. She never liked him. She went to bed with him but she never liked him. So now what do you think about my mother, huh? Did they tell you I broke his jaw and he wanted to have me arrested?"

"What was the fight about?"

"What do you think it was about? He screwed something up for me, something that made a lot of difference. I mean literally, man. He got a girl I knew pregnant. He moved in on me and— Oh Christ!"

"What was her name? Will you tell me that?"

"You go to hell! No way. The cops were taking me away, he had me arrested for breaking his jaw, and I told him I was going to tell them why we were having the fight. Names and everything. He sent his lawyer to get the charges dismissed. I'm not going to get her name dirtied up in this."

"And you haven't seen him since?"

"I didn't say that."

"Where did you go when you left here Thursday?"

"To Richmond. I had to see somebody."

"Your father."

"He wasn't in Richmond."

"How did you know that?"

"He's got deals going in Charlottesville. A shopping center and some apartments. He owes a lot of money he can't straighten out; he spends a lot of his time there."

"He's in trouble because of money?"

"It's nothing he can't—couldn't get out of. He was running short of cash all of a sudden."

"Did you go there to see him?"

"Sure. I went there. He's hard to find."

"But you did find him?"

"I told you. He's hard to find."

"Did you see him yesterday?"

"Yesterday? I don't remember."

"You said you went to Richmond Thursday. Were you in Charlottesville yesterday?"

"What if I was? I had something to do there. Something personal." He and Angus had been standing. Now Brod turned around and sat heavily in a chair in a corner. He leaned forward resting his face in his hands. "Somebody told you they saw me. You knew all along I was there."

Angus did not answer. He did not want Brod to know he didn't know what to say next. He went around the table and found a chair opposite Brod. He waited until Brod raised his head.

"I found out in Charlottesville that he was going to the Lyneses for the cockfights. I've been there a few times, but never to a cockfight. I went out there. It was late, everybody was inside where the fights were going on. I stood outside for a while but I didn't go inside. While I was there maybe half a dozen people came out, but I kept out of sight. I saw him come out. My father, I mean. He went off around the side of the barn."

"He didn't see you?"

"I was standing over behind a car."

"Was there anybody with him?"

"No. I figured he was going around the barn to piss or something, but when he didn't come back after a few minutes I went off there to look for him. There was some kind of a side room off the barn, a kind of shed, with a wide door. I could hear somebody inside, like they were arguing. I mean, somebody was giving somebody else hell."

"Did you see who it was?"

"It was dark inside and outside, too. I heard who I thought was my old man say, 'You give me any trouble I'll have Jack Lynes get rid of you. You watch how you talk.' The other voice said, 'Do what you damn well please. You keep away or I'll kill you, you understand?' Then my old man said, 'Take your hands off me you son of a bitch,' and there was some grunting like they were fighting. One of them came out of the door like he was being pushed and the other one said, 'Somebody should have killed you a long time ago, you filthy bastard.'"

"You know who the other man was?"

"No. My father went back to the cockfights and the other man went off the other way. In a minute he came back with a girl by the arm. He told her to go home, he'd deal with her later. She went off around some cars without saying anything and he went on around the barn to the fights."

"Did you recognize the girl?"

"It was dark, but I could tell she was young. And she was wearing shorts. Really short shorts."

"What time was that?"

"Hell, I wasn't looking at a clock, man. Ten-thirty, or later. Between then and eleven, I guess."

"Did you see anybody else outside?"

"There was some guy standing around a car out there. I didn't pay any attention."

"What did you do then?"

"I went around and looked in the door at the cockfights. My father was sitting down and drinking out of a flask. Mrs. Cumberley was sitting beside him and she reached over to smooth his hair. It was all messed up. He pushed her hand away and said something. They looked like they'd been having a fight about something. You know they're shacking up, don't you?"

"What did you do then?"

"Stood around for a couple of minutes and then left. There wasn't anything I could do. I went back to Charlottesville."

"Whose car did you use?"

"My own, man. They wouldn't let me keep it here, so I left it in Phoebeville at the Exxon station. Bobby Horewood looked after it for me."

"You didn't try to see him again?"

"I knew it didn't make any difference anymore. He wasn't ever going to change. Somebody was going to get him sooner or later, and I knew it didn't have to be me."

"But you went out there to get him?"

"I don't know. That's the truth. I just wanted—the filthy bastard didn't have any right to live." Brod turned around and struck the wall with both fists, beating the wood, then turned and looked straight at Angus. Without warning he began to sob, tears running down to the corners of his mouth. He brushed his face with the palms of his hands, crying without shame. Angus was young enough that it embarrassed him; he got up and went to look out of the window while Brod's sobs changed to words.

"Killing's too good for *him!* Jesus!" His breath was coming in short hard gasps. Through his snuffles he cleared his throat. When his voice was steady he wiped his nose with the back of his hand. "It's okay, man. You never seen a grown man cry before?"

Angus turned around not knowing how to answer Brod's effort at a joke. Brod was wiping his face with a dirty blue bandanna. He blew his nose loudly and cleared his throat, but he did not speak.

"I know it's rough on you, your dad being killed like this. I never knew somebody's father could be like that. But I've got to know. What was it you went looking for him for? It might help us to find out who killed him."

"So you can give him a medal. He ought to get a medal, not the chair."

"Was it something to do with this girl who died last year when she was pregnant?"

"Jesus! He's forty-five years old, for God's sake. I know what they say about him, he's got some kind of animal attraction. Fathers are supposed to tell their sons about sex and all that, right? I mean, we hear it all at school, but the only thing he ever said to me that you call talking about sex? I was fifteen. He told me, 'If you want to make out, you got to ask. All you have to do is ask.' That's the way it was with her. All he had to do was ask." Brod was about to cry again. "She just said, 'Sure.' Just like that."

"Does anybody else know about them?"

"I don't know. I only found out—I followed her once from the restaurant where she worked. She'd moved and wouldn't tell me where. My old man picked her up and drove her to this place on the Southside. Some nights I'd sit outside in my car and watch them come in. I didn't want her to know I was following her. One night I was there when my old man came out like he was in a hurry, and the next day—" Brod stopped. His voice broke and he had to try twice before he spoke again. "The next day—I heard she had died."

"Is that when you had the fight with him?"

"He wasn't even sorry!" He pounded the table with both fists. "I should have killed him then. He was scared to death but he wasn't sorry. I would have beat him to death, if that secretary hadn't called the police!"

"You weren't arrested?"

"He knew I'd make trouble, real trouble."

"You didn't want to make trouble for him, after all that?"

"Well Christ! He was my father. I wish now I'd made him arrest me."

"You think he killed that girl?"

"She died because of him. You ask Annabel. She'll tell you. Ask her what she told me."

"I talked to her. She told me about the girl; she said she died of a botched abortion."

"She's studying medicine. She knows about all kinds of things like that. It's disgusting. It made me sick; I don't want to talk about it. Ask her."

"Will you tell me the girl's name?"

"No way, man. It doesn't have anything to do with this. You keep her name out of it."

"If I give you a name, will you say if she's the one?"

"Nobody knows but me and—and he's dead."

"Was her name Cumberley? Was that her name?"

Brod opened his mouth but nothing came out. He went fast out of the office and slammed the door behind him.

CHAPTER 16

Angus found Annabel in a corner of the child care building half an hour later. She had a one-year-old child in her lap, rocking it gently in an old-fashioned rocking chair. She shushed him as he came in, got up, and took the child to another room. "I just wanted to hold one of them for a while," she said when she returned. "I don't like children much, but babies. That's another thing."

"Brod said you could tell me something I need to know."

"Ask me. I'll tell you if I'm going to tell you."

"You remember I asked you about embolisms?"

"I wondered what you were onto."

"It was something else I had heard earlier that made me ask you. I didn't know it had anything to do with Mark Nailles. I didn't know then; Brod told me about the girl who died. He said I should ask you what you told him."

"I didn't know it was going to bug him out of his mind like that."

"Like what?"

"Like he'd go off and kill his old man. That's what you think he did, don't you?"

"I don't know. I'm just trying to find out what happened."

Annabel laughed unhumorously. "You want facts, I can give you some facts. If you think you're ready for them. Facts are facts, man; people better be ready for them all the time."

She got up from the rocking chair and gestured for Angus to follow. They walked across the compound to her room and Angus stood beside the door while Annabel pulled a file folder from a shelf and rummaged through a stack of papers.

"Last winter when I was reading some old medical journals I came across something. I made some photocopies because it was related to a class I was taking. Thank God it never came up in class. Those smart-ass chauvinists would have made it one big laugh. It's not funny, but those chauvinist pig doctors—here. You don't have to read it here. It won't embarrass me, but I don't know about you. You embarrass easily." Angus knew that she was baiting him.

Angus took the papers. There were four sheets clipped together. He looked at the caption on the first sheet: "Fatal Air Embolism Caused by Bizarre Sexual Behavior During Pregnancy." He glanced at the subhead below and felt his face getting red.

"What it says—" Annabel said.

"I see what it says." Angus felt her watching him, heard the slyness in her voice. He folded the papers and slipped them in his pocket.

"The doctor who wrote that document saw half a dozen cases where pregnant women died of air embolism after their husbands or boyfriends had played around like that." She saw his expression and laughed. "Don't worry, it only happens if you're pregnant."

"I'll take it along and read it."

"It's full of medical terms; it's not what you think, dirty. What it says is sometimes air can get into her circulatory system. When that happens she dies, snap, just like that, when the air gets to her heart."

Angus felt himself sweating. He did not want to stand there talking about things like that with Annabel, and he was thinking what he might have to tell Mr. Cumberley. "When did you tell Brod about this?"

"I think it was last Wednesday. He was unloading it all on me about what a bastard his old man was, what had happened to this girl. I looked it up in the library and made some copies of it and showed it to him. It really shook him." She chuckled sourly, savoring the memory. "Stuff like this can shake lots of people." She was suddenly serious. "If more law people like you knew things like this, we could get at the pigs like Brod's old man."

"Wouldn't a doctor know about this when he made an autopsy?"

"They just put it down to a botched abortion probably self-induced. So the doctors won't be blamed. Read it and you'll see how tricky autopsies can be, if you don't know what to look for."

"Did you show this to anybody else?"

She looked down at her fingers, turning her hands to examine her nails. "I passed it around to one or two I thought ought to be interested."

"Who'd you think would be interested in something like this?"

"Medical people, law people. Like that. It's something they ought to know about, don't you think?"

"Depends on why they have to know." He folded the paper and put it in his pocket.

Angus left her and went back to the shed, hoping that Moon would be there. He wanted to forget all the unpleasantness of Mark Nailles. She was not there. Vee said that she had gone to bed. Angus hung around for a while, then said good night.

In his room he read the article through twice. The medical and technical words meant little to him, but the point was clear. Annabel had prompted Brod to think that his father was responsible for Emily Cumberley's death and he had gone looking for him for two days and had found him the night he was murdered. Angus went to sleep wondering if there was any truth in what Annabel was implying and what Cumberley would do if he knew about Mark Nailles and his daughter.

CHAPTER 17

For Saturday night things had been quiet. A woman near Gabbles had complained about kids on dirt bikes; somebody reported a car parked outside Penstevens' grocery store at Adam's Union; a carful of teenagers had driven into a ditch near Petite Grange; a horse was loose near Hullet's Tavern; a man was seen prowling around some trailers at the Sunnyview Trailer Court. A deer had jumped in front of a car on the Devil's Marker road; the deer was killed and the car had to be towed. The driver suffered some cuts and was treated at the scene.

"You got a funeral at Mount Tabor Church this afternoon at two-thirty," the night deputy told him. "You have to handle the traffic where it crosses Fifty-nine. And the sheriff wants you to stop by his house soon as you can. He's got some wild hair up his ass about that killing over at Copperfields." He put his coffee cup down. "I hear the dead man was a bigger rounder than the sheriff. That's hard to believe."

Angus shrugged. He didn't look forward to seeing the sheriff.

Mrs. Rowe came to the door before he could knock. She was dressed for church in a flowered dress and elaborate hat. She was a heavy woman, forty pounds overweight. The girlish prettiness of her face had hardened into an expression of eternal Christian forbearance. She was sustained in her lot as the sheriff's wife by the unstinting sympathy of her friends in the Missionary Society, several of whom knew how truly the sympathy was due. Jennie would not have left the sheriff for all the vengeance in heaven.

"He's out back," she told Angus. "You can go through the kitchen here."

He found Rowe stretched on a couch on the back porch. The sheriff winced painfully as he shifted his weight from one hip to the other. "Panthorpe gave me something for the pain but it don't do a goddamn bit of good. Tell you, boy, you ever have trouble with your back you never get over it. The way Jennie acts you'd think I was putting it all on. You reckon she knows how I got it?"

Angus made a platitude about taking it easy being the only way to cure it. He did not answer the question. They both knew the answer.

"How the hell can I take it easy with this Lynes thing hanging over me? Panthorpe told me yesterday afternoon he looked at Nailles's body before he sent if off for the autopsy. It was some kind of sharp instrument ripped his clothes up. Lots of puncture wounds in his belly. Panthorpe said they looked like they was superficial, but there was other deeper ones in his chest and belly. He found one of them cockspur gaffs stuck in his gut. You saw the bloody mess it made. Panthorpe said whoever done it must have jumped on him and just ripped him up. Them little bitty things is sharp as hell."

"I've never seen one."

"Don't seem they'd be long enough, but they sure as hell can kill a chicken, and it looks like one of them killed this one, too. Panthorpe said he'll have a report for us maybe tomorrow. If it was a gaff was used, we got to check out everybody there that was handling them birds. That means Bobby Horewood, and Sam Tilke from Lovettsville, and Harry Irons. You can't make me believe old Harry'd do a thing like that. And there was a couple of fellows from up in Madison County. Pat Rillbon will know their names."

"He's sure it was the gaff that was used?"

"He thought some of the wounds was too deep for a gaff, but he's not sure."

Angus told him about the hatchet and how Peaches said she had found it. He didn't tell him who Peaches was with behind the barn Friday night. He'd save that for another time.

"Didn't look like no hatchet was used, to me. You better get it to the lab anyway. And you get with Pat Rillbon and find out who else had chickens there and was handling. Find out if any of them is missing a gaff."

Angus didn't know how he was going to manage all of that by himself, but he nodded.

"What about that boy—he turn up yet?"

Angus told him how he had found Brod at Sweet Valley; he went quickly through Brod's version of where he had been, what he had learned about the fight between Brod and his father. He did not tell him who the girl was or what Annabel had given him.

"That's a good night's work. You got a confession out of him yet?"

"He's not in custody, Sheriff. I didn't have any reason to arrest him."

The sheriff tried to sit up, winced, and eased back down. "Reason? Christ's sake, Bealle, the little bastard went hunting for him for two days. You got proved bad blood between them; the old man was screwing the boy's girlfriend. He was at the scene the night he was murdered. You got motive, you got opportunity. All you got to do is find out where he got the gaff. What else do you got to have?"

"It's not enough, Sheriff."

"Then you make it enough. You get your ass over to Sweet Valley and you put him in custody. We'll make it enough to put him in the chair."

"What about Rillbon? Brod Nailles heard Rillbon and Nailles arguing in the shed. He threatened Nailles. Told him to stay away from Peaches."

"If Pat Rillbon killed everybody who ever messed around with his daughter half the county would be in the cemetery. Including you, boy."

"That's not so, Sheriff."

"Then it ain't for not trying. You do like I tell you. Put that boy in the lockup, charge him with something if it's only being a material witness. You hold him till I can get back." He squinted his eyes and peered at his deputy. "There's something you ain't told me yet, boy. You holding something back?"

"I told you everything important. Some details, maybe."

"Details is what makes police work, you know that. You studied all them classes, didn't you?"

"Sure, Sheriff."

"Then let's hear the details."

Angus pulled the photocopies from his shirt pocket and unfolded them. "This girl who died last year; they put it down to an embolism related to a botched abortion. That's air in the veins, Sheriff. It was probably what happened. But there's this woman at Sweet Valley who's studying medicine. She showed this article to Brod Nailles. Something from a medical magazine." He handed Rowe the sheets.

"My glasses is inside. You tell me what it says."

Angus gave him a quick summary, trying to keep it as matter-of-fact as he could.

"You mean a woman can die from— Son of a bitch!"

"I think this woman had her own reasons for showing this to Brod. But it was the thing that set him off."

The sheriff wasn't listening. "Well, ain't that something. This girl who died? Did you get her name?"

"I'll have to check that out." If Angus could avoid it he was not going to have the sheriff know that it was Cumberley's daughter.

"You check, and you lock that boy up if he ain't already long gone from here."

"What about Rillbon?"

"Rillbon's a good man. He's got his problems but he ain't got the guts to kill somebody over that little slut of his. We got a case against the boy. This way we keep it in the family, we don't make trouble for people like Jack Lynes."

"Nailles was the one involved in that business with Mrs. Rillbon. That might give Rillbon reason to kill him, if he was trying something with Peaches, after what happened to her mother."

"All that business sort of killed his spirit, you might say. He's different now. No, you find that boy."

Angus was silent for a minute. "There's somebody else. Somebody who got the same kind of business from Nailles a long time ago."

"Yeah? Who's that?"

"The Lynes's cook has a daughter. She's visiting her mother at Copperfields. She lives in New York. She hates Nailles; she said he raped her when she was sixteen."

The sheriff made a noise half snort, half chuckle. "Raped her?

Like saying you raped a fish, catching it. All you got to do is bait the hook."

"Dammit, Sheriff. I told you that because she's there and she might have a motive. She's a decent woman."

"Now wouldn't that beat all, if it turned out the cook and her gal done it? That way it wouldn't make no difference to nobody but Mrs. Lynes. She'd just lose herself a cook."

"She might have a motive, but I don't think she did it."

"Hey, boy, sounds like you got something about this gal. That so, boy?"

"I'm trying to do my job, Sheriff. I'm supposed to uphold the law, treat everybody the same. Just because somebody's black—"

"Don't tell me what the law is, Bealle. You just get out there and do your job. You find somebody, I don't give a damn who it is, and you lock them up for killing that gamarooching sport. You hear me? You want to mess with some color, you do it on your own time."

Angus turned and went down the steps and around the house without answering. He knew that if he stayed he might kick the sheriff off his couch. He sat in his car while his anger subsided. He was sitting there when the rescue squad dispatcher called him.

"This is car seven. What you got?"

"It's over there at Copperfields, Angus. You better get over there fast. They turned up another dead one. This time it's Lynes himself."

CHAPTER 18

Angus helped the sheriff ease into his patrol car. While Rowe shouted into the radio, Angus drove with his foot on the floor toward Copperfields, his siren screaming.

"You call Skinker, if you can't get him, get anybody else you can find," the sheriff bellowed. "Tell him to get over to Sweet Valley and take that Nailles boy into custody, bring him to Lynes's place." He handed the microphone to Angus, cursing the day in general and the pain in his back in particular. "We going to get this thing settled, and I mean today."

"You going to charge Brod Nailles, Sheriff?"

"I'm going to hold his ass in jail until I can pin it on him good. Or on somebody. What the hell's he doing, killing a man like Jack Lynes?"

The rescue squad ambulance was in the driveway near the kitchen door, its red lights flashing, when Angus pulled up. Three members of the squad in blue coverall uniforms stood at a corner of the kitchen near a gate leading to the lawn behind the house. Nick Mathers, Fossy Glove, and Biston Barrell, in the same kind of bright golf clothes they had worn the day before, were standing with them. Pat Rillbon and Jeff were to one side, leaning against the pickup truck.

The sheriff made Angus help him gingerly from the patrol car and follow him to the gate. Rowe nodded stiffly to the squad men and turned to their leader. "All right, Billy. Let's see what we got here."

Billy Hogshead, a slight intense man with an acne-scarred face, led them through the gate and along a brick path. The others, failing orders from the sheriff to stay where they were, followed. They went up wide brick steps to the terrace which stretched across the rear façade of the house. The steps and the terrace were edged with a balustrade; iron urns planted with ferns marked the corners where the railing turned at the top of the steps. Angus saw furled canvas umbrellas over metal tables and groups of iron chairs and lounges covered in bright canvas. Through a French door he saw Amy Cumberley watching as they climbed the steps.

The rescue squad had covered Lynes's body with a blanket. Billy reached down and pulled it back. Lynes lay sprawled across a wide padded lounge, his head and shoulders against the flagstone floor, arms twisted under him. His hips and legs lay diagonally across the lounge. There was a dark mess running down from a deep gash in his neck. Drying blood had glued his face and hair to the stone. A large black insect scurried away as Billy threw back the blanket.

"Been dead some time," the sheriff said to nobody, and then to Angus, "You go call Panthorpe. You tell him I need him over here. This time we ain't sending no body away until he's looked at it right here. Don't let him give you any crap about it. You understand?"

Angus nodded but did not move.

"There's a telephone in the kitchen," Fossy Glove said.

"All right now, who found him?" The sheriff looked around at the three men. Nick Mathers raised a hand.

"I did, Sheriff. About thirty, forty minutes ago."

Angus waited to hear the rest of it.

"Didn't I tell you to call Panthorpe?" Rowe demanded. "Then get the hell in there and do it."

As Angus went down the steps and around to the kitchen door, he heard Mathers saying, "I went out for a walk earlier this morning, I guess I was gone about an hour; when I came back . . ."

Dr. Panthorpe was as disagreeable as Angus expected he would be, but he promised to get there as soon as possible. Maggie Allan was not in the kitchen, but used cups and plates in the sink and half a melon on the counter told him that someone had prepared breakfast. A clock over the sink said it was nine thirty-seven, five minutes slower than Angus's watch.

The sheriff was talking to Biston Barrell when Angus returned. Someone had put a blanket over Lynes's body and the group had moved to the balustrade near one of the urns. The two squad men were seated on the rail, their feet dangling. Pat and Jeff Rillbon had not followed them from the driveway and were nowhere to be seen.

"Everybody was uptight about Mark's death," Biston Barrell was saying. "It wasn't much of an evening. Kenyon of course had canceled the cocktail party she was giving. Some of the girls wanted to get up a bridge game but it didn't work out. I mean, we were all on edge, snapping at each other over nothing at all. Jack had been moody all night. He just kept on drinking. He and Kenyon quarreled about it. She tried to make him stop and he told her he could drink all he goddamn well pleased. After a while everybody just drifted off to bed. Jack stayed downstairs watching some late show on television. He was so sloshed by that time I don't see how he made much sense out of anything he was watching."

Nick Mathers cut in. "The television was still going this morning when I came down."

"Who was the last one saw him?" the sheriff demanded.

"I suppose I did," Nick said. "I wasn't in much of a mood to go to bed. Jack walked out here on the terrace. Said he was going to stay up awhile. Mark's death was getting to him. After all, they had been friends once."

"That's right," Fossy Glove said. "He was way off his game yesterday. Matter of fact, we all were."

"Could see how you would be," Rowe said. The tone was respectful. The sheriff saw no irony in his words. "He say anything would make you think he knew something? I mean, something might make somebody want to kill him?"

"When I told him last night he ought to go to bed," Nick Mathers said. "He said he didn't want to. He was going to stay up and watch television. 'I keep thinking about that boy,' he said."

"The boy!" the sheriff pounced. "I said all along it was the boy. What else did he say?"

"I supposed he meant Mark's son. 'He did it to that boy,' was what he said. I suppose he meant that Mark had driven the boy to it."

"That's right, Sheriff," Barrell said. "He said the same thing to me earlier, while we were playing golf."

"So that was what got you two so upset," Fossy Glove said. "He wouldn't tell me what it was."

"He—it—I told him he was on the wrong track, he ought to leave it to the police. He wasn't—well, he was almost getting intemperate."

The sheriff turned to Angus. "You found the boy last night. I told you you should have taken him in, but you're too stupid to see it." He looked about at his audience. "Said he didn't have enough evidence, for Christ's sake." He jerked his head toward Lynes's body. "Now he's got another one. Well, I got a man on his way out there to Sweet Valley, he'll get him, if he's still there." He looked hard at Angus who stared back at him defiantly. Rowe was playing to his audience, but Angus was not going to be the scapegoat.

"It doesn't make any sense that Brod would want to kill Jack Lynes," Fossy Glove said. "Why would he want to do that?"

"Perhaps he knew Jack had seen him?" Barrell's voice was tentative. "He was wandering around, and he walked back to the house after the fights were over."

"We'll know when we catch the son of a bitch." Rowe turned to Nick Mathers. "What time was it when you left him?"

"About eleven-thirty, maybe later. It wasn't twelve, I'm pretty sure."

"And what time was it you talked to the boy?" the sheriff demanded of Angus.

"About ten-thirty."

The sheriff nodded, satisfied. "You let him go, boy."

For over half an hour the sheriff continued what seemed to Angus a rambling and aimless questioning without establishing more than a few general agreements, after which they all moved into the house. Angus tried to sort out what he had learned.

The golf game had gone badly. Jack Lynes had been in a foul mood, which they attributed to his hangover from the night before and the drinks he had had that morning. The talk kept coming back to Mark Nailles. They all knew that Nailles was having cash-flow problems with his businesses. The violence with which Nailles had been cut indicated a spur-of-the-moment loss of temper or a sudden reaction to something that had brought it on. They tried to reconstruct the events of the fatal night, but they could agree only that several times during the evening Mark Nailles had left the cockfights to go outside. Biston Barrell had gone to inspect the cocks in their cages and to talk to some of the handlers. Barrell had got his trousers bloodied from a wayward fighting cock and Amy Cumberley had suffered the same damage. Jack Lynes had wandered outside for a breath of fresh air, but nobody could remember exactly when during the evening. While they all agreed with the sheriff that Brod Nailles might be a likely candidate, none of them had seen him at the barn on Friday night.

They returned from their golf game late Saturday afternoon. Kenyon Lynes spent most of the afternoon telephoning to cancel the cocktail party she had planned. After dinner there had been some desultory bridge, but everybody was on edge and by eleven-thirty they had all retired except Jack Lynes. Sally Carter Barrell, the dead man's sister, had spent much of the afternoon on the telephone, trying to determine what should be done about funeral arrangements. Nothing could be decided until the autopsy had been completed. She complained of headaches and stayed in her room through dinner.

All of them had planned to leave Sunday morning after breakfast. Nick Mathers said that he and Lois had talked of leaving Saturday but had stayed on at Jack's insistence. It was clear that things were not going well between them. They kept the room between them, responded separately to questions, and did not speak to each other. Nobody said they had noticed anything unusual about Jack, except his drinking. "And that," Lois Mathers said dryly, "wasn't that unusual."

Charlotte Glove came downstairs to say that she had gotten Kenyon settled and quiet, but she had nothing to add to the events of the evening.

Jepson's hearse drove up three minutes before Dr. Panthorpe arrived. The sheriff sent the rescue squad back to their base. Panthorpe grunted as he tried to kneel his bulk down beside Lynes's body, gave up, and turned to Rowe and to Angus. "Get him up here where I can take a look," he ordered. Rowe tossed his head at Angus and Jepson. The undertaker stepped forward and reached down, beckoning to Angus to get on the other side.

Angus felt his stomach turn at the notion of touching the bloody body but he reached down and grasped Lynes's shirt. They heaved back and Angus knew he would vomit if he did not turn away. The body came up and away from the bloody stones, its rigor holding the limbs stiff in the positon in which they had lain. Gluey strings of jellied blood rose as Jepson flung the dead man across the lounge.

Angus made for the balustrade and leaned over, throwing up. He hung there, staring through wet eyes at the ground below, his body hot with shame.

When he turned around, wiping the sweat from his face and tasting the bitterness of his vomit, he heard Panthorpe say, "No question. Somebody severed the carotid and the jugular with something sharp, a knife or razor."

"What about a gaff? Could it have been a cockspur?" Angus put his handkerchief away under the disgusted stare of the sheriff.

"Wasn't stabbed, he was cut," Panthorpe said. Lynes's stiffened body lay grotesquely angled as the doctor poked at the wound with a gloved finger. He stood up. "All right, Jepson, you can have it. Get it on to the lab like the other one, soon as you can."

"I got a funeral this afternoon, Doctor. Old Mrs. Anderson, over at Mount Tabor Church."

"Yes, heard she had died. Wasn't my patient. You take him along, do whatever you have to."

The sheriff turned to Angus. "You got anything else to do besides puking, you better get at it. I want to be at the lockup when Skinker brings the boy in. You drive me home so I can get my patrol car. I'll get the doc here to give me another shot so I can get around. Okay, Doc?"

Panthorpe said he'd meet him at his office. They left Jepson and his assistant to clear away the body and Angus waited while Panthorpe took the sheriff into his clinic and gave him an injection. On the way to the sheriff's house Angus got his instructions.

"Before you handle that funeral this afternoon, you go back there to Copperfields, you talk to Pat Rillbon, find out what he can tell you about those gaffs. He might know something. That is, if you can stop puking long enough to talk to him."

CHAPTER 19

At Copperfields, Angus parked near the kitchen door and walked through the garden to the terrace. Beginning in a corner near the kitchen, he searched methodically across the terrace until he came to the railing. He pushed through the shrubbery on either side of the steps; the ivy under the heavy planting was thick and his sleeve was stained to the elbow from running his hand through the matted leaves. Over the scent of the green leaves he caught the sourness of his earlier vomiting. He brushed the memory of his earlier weakness aside.

When he had checked the shrubbery on both sides of the steps, he climbed them, checking the rail opposite the one he had followed down. He parted the fronds of the ferns in the urns at the top of the steps. Before he returned to his car, he went over the terrace again but found nothing.

The pickup truck was in front of Rillbon's house but his automobile was gone. Angus knew that Mrs. Rillbon was at church. His parents went to the same church, and Mrs. Rillbon never missed a service. His mother sometimes commented on Selma Rillbon's uncompromising disapproval of what other people did and he wondered what she must know about her daughter. His mother must have known what the sheriff had told him about Mrs. Rillbon, but she had never mentioned it. What had happened to her might explain her rigid attitudes.

He found Pat Rillbon setting out tomato plants in the garden behind his house. Rillbon did not stop working as Angus came through the gate. His face was tired and worn. "Everybody else has gone off to church."

"I guess this hits you pretty hard, working here for so long."

"I'm still working here, Angus. Things go on, you know." He stood up, pushed the flat along the row, and knelt again.

"Doctor Panthorpe said Nailles was ripped up pretty bad

around the guts and belly and he found a steel cockspur stuck in him. Mr. Lynes might have been cut the same way. Did you hear anybody Friday night say he was missing any gaffs?"

Rillbon dug a hole, pressed the earth around a plant. "Nobody said anything to me."

"It's not something you'd leave lying around."

"Wouldn't say so, no."

"Could somebody identify one if he saw it was his?"

"I'd think probably they could. It's like any tool you use, you get to know it."

"Do you keep any around here?"

"There's half a dozen pair over there in the barn, been there since Mr. Fess's time. I usually keep them locked up."

"Any of them missing?"

"Haven't looked. Bobby Horewood was using some of them Friday night. I leave it to him to put them back."

"I'd like to take a look at them."

"Soon as I finish this row, Angus. You grab that hose and put some water on those tomatoes while I finish up."

Angus saw that Rillbon was fighting to keep from showing what Jack Lynes's death had done to him. He followed him down the row, dribbling water on the newly set tomatoes. "I understand you and Mark Nailles had some words over there Friday night." He kept his voice even and respectful.

"Who told you that, Angus?" Rillbon's tone was rather like Angus's father's when as a boy Angus had made some outlandish statement that needed to be gently but firmly put down. Amused but disbelieving.

"Somebody saw you, Mr. Rillbon."

"You think I killed him, Angus?"

"I don't know who killed him, Mr. Rillbon. That's what I'm trying to find out."

"The sheriff send you here to ask me that?"

"No, sir. But he knows about it."

"How does he know?"

"I told him."

"How do you know?"

"I told you. Somebody saw you."

Rillbon planted two tomato plants without speaking. "There's no use my acting like we don't know what this is all about," he said finally. "I'm not a damn fool, and I guess you're not either." He put the last of the tomato plants in the ground, threw the trowel into the empty plant flat, and stood up. Angus pulled the hose along, ran water over the last of the tomatoes, and cut the water off at the nozzle. Rillbon waited silently until he finished.

"You've been around here all your life, Angus; you've heard all the talk. About—about Selma, and what happened."

Angus shook his head. "No, sir. I never knew anything until this morning. The sheriff told me."

"I should have guessed he'd tell you. It's not the sort of thing he could forget. What did he tell you, exactly?"

"That there was some kind of trouble over at the University at a dance. Mark Nailles was involved, and Mr. Lynes's uncle got him out of trouble. Lynes was in it too."

"That's all? None of the dirty details?"

"No, sir."

"There were plenty of dirty details." Rillbon turned away, put a hand on a fence post, and looked down at the ground. It was a long minute before Angus realized that Rillbon was crying. He had seen more men cry in the last two days than he had in his life. Rillbon turned around, wiped his face and eyes with a hand, and blew his nose into a blue bandanna. "It still hurts, Angus. Not just what happened then, but what's happened ever since. I loved Selma then, and I suppose I still do, but it's different now. I was just out of high school. We'd been going steady for two years. I never had another girl. She was pretty as could be, but Bushanna County was real country then. We'd never been outside the county except for some basketball games and once when the whole junior class went to Williamsburg on a bus trip.

"Jack Lynes used to come to Copperfields to visit his uncle. I worked here before I graduated from high school. We got to know each other. He got to know Selma too. Then one time he asked her to go to a dance at the University. He was a decent fellow but I didn't want her to go, but she said she'd never get another chance like that and her mother said she was old enough to make up her own mind. She said it would be good for her to get out and see how other people lived. Jack Lynes didn't mean any harm; he just wanted her to have a good time and thought it would be fun for her.

"She promised me nothing was going to happen, she just wanted to go to a big college dance. I should have known what would happen. She'd never had a drink in her life. Everybody was drinking, and she went along with the crowd and before she knew it she was drunk and they—Christ Almighty!"

"It's okay, Mr. Rillbon. You don't have to tell me anything more."

"No. You had best know. She was in a hospital for two weeks and then she was in this mental place for almost a year. I'd go to see her and she'd just sit there. When she got better finally I took her home and we got married." For the first time he looked directly at Angus. "I know what they all say. Jack Lynes's uncle bought me off, gave me a house and a job just so I'd marry her. That's not true. I did it because I loved her and I wanted to make it up to her for letting her get into all that. I suppose if I'd been more of a man then, and even now, I'd have taken her and gone somewhere far off. Here I am working for Jack Lynes and people think I'm just chicken-livered. I got over hating Lynes a long time ago for what he did, because I decided it wasn't all his fault. Some of the fault was his, but Selma said he did what he could to stop it. She was the one who wanted to stay here."

"You've made a good life here, Mr. Rillbon."

"What I don't understand is how he could stay friends with a man like Nailles after what he did. It took him ten years before he quit being friends with Nailles."

"Was there something that happened that made them stop being friends?"

"Not that I know of. The Lyneses are decent people; they just got disgusted with the way he acted, I suppose." Rillbon pulled his hat down. "So now what you want to know is did I kill the two of them."

"I just want to find out who killed them. You didn't tell me yesterday that you were with Mark Nailles in that shed or that you had an argument with him."

"No, I didn't. There's no use kidding ourselves, Angus. You know what the argument was about. I'm her father, but I'm not a blind man. I know what she is, and I saw the way he was looking at her, the way she was watching him. And I saw him get up and follow her when she went out of the barn. But I stopped him before he caught up with her. There are some things I can't stop, but I was going to stop that." He walked the length of the garden to the gate, bent, and turned off the water at the tap. "I'll tell you before you find out somewhere else. Jack Lynes has been giving Peaches presents and money. It hasn't gone any further than that, and he probably was just being kind. But that's another reason why you've got to think I might have killed him." He closed the gate behind him and stood beside it. "It was Mr. Cumberley who told you about Nailles and me." There was no question in his tone, just confirmation of one more fact.

"No, sir. He wasn't there."

"Yes he was, Angus. He was standing near the barn when I came around from the shed."

"You sure it was him?"

"You think I don't know him?"

"But it wasn't Mr. Cumberley who saw you. Wasn't him who told me, I mean."

They walked around to the front of the house. Mrs. Rillbon, Jeff, and Peaches were getting out of their automobile. Jeff nodded at Angus and went into the house. Mrs. Rillbon, in a blue dress and dark blue hat, carried a Bible and a purse in one hand. The dark circles under her eyes were emphasized by the midday sun. Peaches's dress did nothing to conceal her lush youth.

"It's a terrible thing, Angus," Mrs. Rillbon said. "I've been praying that you will find the one who did these terrible things. It makes me sick." She turned her head and put her hand against her mouth. Her eyes were wet with tears. Pat Rillbon put a hand on her arm; she tensed and drew away.

"At least it's something happening," Peaches said petulantly. "It breaks the monotony of this boring place."

Without warning her mother spun around and struck her against the head with the Bible. "You stop that before it's too late! I've told you before!" She ran across the grass and up the steps to the front door. Pat Rillbon started after her then stopped and turned to his daughter.

"You whore! That's what I've raised. A whore. You pay heed to your mother! You'll end up like her, only there won't be somebody to take you in. Nobody, do you hear?"

CHAPTER 20

Peaches ran across the lawn and up the steps, her hand against her head where her mother had struck her. Angus waited until she was inside before he said, "About those spurs, Mr. Rillbon."

"I'll get my keys."

Angus saw Peaches watching from a front window when Rillbon returned. He followed Rillbon to the barn, where he broke the seal and pushed the wide doors open. The interior had a rancid odor, part chicken manure, part stale air. In a corner two dead roosters had settled into a dull mat of feathers. Iridescent blue flies buzzed around them. They were beginning to stink.

Rillbon led him to a small room behind the seats. Its walls were covered with photographs of fighting cocks, faded pages torn from cockfighting magazines. There were two chairs and a worn table against one wall. A small wall cupboard with an open padlock hung over the table. Rillbon removed the padlock and swung the door open. On a shelf were half a dozen small leather kits. Rillbon picked one up, opened it, and took out a pair of steel spurs. Angus accepted them gingerly, avoiding the needle-sharp points.

The steel was surgical quality, about two inches long, curving from the base to a sharp tapered point. At the base of the spur was a crossbar with an open eye which fit over the natural spur and was lashed to the leg with a leather thong. A fighting cock fitted with a pair of these steel spurs could sink its gaffs into an opponent to the hilt.

"Up north," Rillbon said, "they use spurs that are shorter than these. Farther south they're longer."

"Do you keep them locked up here?"

"I left the box open for Bobby Horewood. He uses them when

he's handling birds. I told him to lock them up when he was finished but it looks like he forgot."

"Bobby Horewood was using these spurs?"

"He handles for Jack Lynes now and then. We don't keep many birds anymore." One by one Rillbon took down the spurs and showed them to Angus. There were five kits. Reaching up to the top shelf he took down a sixth. Instead of sharp points the spurs had razor-sharp edges, like a surgeon's scalpel. "These are called slashers. It's a dirty business using them. Makes a fast bloody fight. A bird can cut another's head off with these. Nobody around here uses them but they're used frequently, I'm told, down in the Caribbean. Cuba, Haiti, places like that." He reached up, felt on the shelf. "Used to be two pair here, but there's only one now."

"There's a pair missing?"

"Could have been gone for a long time. I don't check this out more than once a year."

"When was the last time you saw the other pair?"

"God, I don't know. A year or more, at least. Maybe longer."

"Do you keep this cupboard locked?"

"I really don't notice. Bobby borrows these things and I usually leave it up to him to keep it locked."

"But you said you unlocked it for Bobby last Friday."

"Sometime Friday afternoon. But I leave it open sometimes for months unless I remember to lock it. To be honest, I don't pay a lot of attention anymore. Except for this hack fight every spring, there's not any fighting here anymore. When Mr. Fess Lynes was living there were fights all the time, through the winter and spring. After this time of year the cocks begin molting. The fights used to go on for two days at a time. He was ninety-one and blind when he died, but he kept them up."

"My dad said he used to have a lot of wild parties here."

"That was before my time. He's been dead now for about twelve years. Before that he had slowed down on that sort of thing. He used to have all kinds of parties here."

"My dad said he'd bring women down from Washington and Baltimore. He'd grease a pole in here, put two hundred dollars at the top of it, and they'd all watch the naked women try to scramble up the pole."

"That was a long time ago."

"He said something happened, they had to take one of the women to the hospital in Charlottesville."

"Times change, Angus."

"People don't, Mr. Rillbon."

Rillbon listened without expression, then put the leather kits back on the shelves. "We'll shut this barn down for good now. Should be six pairs of gaffs, two slashers, if I remember right."

"That means a pair of gaffs and a pair of slashers are missing."

"Bobby might have kept a pair of the gaffs but he wouldn't have any use for the slashers."

"Doctor Panthorpe found a gaff in Nailles's body. Could you identify it if it was one of yours?"

"I'd know the kit, but I don't know about the gaff."

"The other men who were fighting cocks Friday night. They'd have gaffs too."

"I know most of them. The sheriff knows them. But there's no reason why one of them would want to kill Jack Lynes, or that other fellow."

"One of them might have a gaff missing."

"It's more likely somebody took them out of here. This room was open, so was the cabinet. Anybody could have got to them." Rillbon looked hard at Angus. "Including me. That's what you're thinking."

"There are people who would say you had reason. If the sheriff wasn't so dead set on pinning it on young Nailles, he'd be saying it too."

Pat Rillbon closed the door of the cupboard and snapped the lock shut. He walked out of the office, waited for Angus, and pulled the door shut behind him. Outside he waited while Angus put the seal back on the doors. "I gave up wanting to kill them a long time ago. I never forgot what they did. Now it looks like it's starting all over again with Peaches. You know what she is, Angus. The whole county knows. I can't talk about it to her mother. She won't listen. She doesn't want to admit it. When she does finally admit it, it's going to kill her."

"I'm sorry, Mr. Rillbon. Whatever happens, I've got to find out who killed those men."

"You do what you have to do, Angus. When the time comes."

They walked back to the house. Peaches was at the top of the steps on the porch, watching for them. She had changed her clothes and was wearing a black T-shirt and white shorts. She was barefooted. She looked at her father coolly as they came up to the house.

"I just came out here to tell you Mama said dinner is about ready."

"All right, Peaches."

"She said to ask Angus if he wants to stay and have dinner with us."

Rillbon looked at Angus and Angus looked away, knowing that the older man read what was in his mind. Would a policeman sit at the table of a man he thought was a murderer?

"How about it, Angus? You're welcome to stay."

"Jeff's not here," Peaches said. "He's gone over to Charlottesville. You can take his place, Angus."

"Sure, Mr. Rillbon. Thank you. I'd like to."

He followed them through the house to the kitchen. Mrs. Rillbon had set four plates at a table by a window. Her face was drawn, her thin mouth pressed tight. When they were seated she bowed her head. Peaches ducked hers but watched Angus through her thick lashes.

"Oh Lord, we thank You for this bounty which You have provided, and for Your promise of salvation. Remove the terrible cloud that hangs over this house and the house of those near to us, and bring Thy terrible swift sword Oh Jesus to the one who has done these deeds, no matter where Thy sword may fall. Save us from all our sins in the name of Sweet Jesus. Amen."

Angus through his half-closed lids saw Peaches flash a quick look at her father when her mother mentioned the vengeful sword. The intensity of Mrs. Rillbon's voice belied her tired look.

Peaches's head popped up at the amen and her hand shot out toward the basket of bread. The Rillbon Sunday meal was one that Angus knew. With variations it was what his mother served, ready when the family returned from church. Cold fried chicken, macaroni salad, something molded in green or orange gelatin. Angus and Pat Rillbon made a few inconsequential tries at conversation, avoiding the thing that was on all their minds, but Selma and Peaches made no effort to join in, so they fell silent and ate.

Mrs. Rillbon was at a counter cutting slices of lemon meringue pie when Peaches finally had something to say. "I was talking to Ethel Sue Shufflet at church, she said if people knew what the sheriff was doing when his back went out he wouldn't get re-elected. Do you know what he was doing at that precise moment, Angus?"

Mrs. Rillbon turned around, the knife in her hand. "You stop that talk now. I've told you before—"

"Oh, Mama. Everybody knows what the sheriff's like. Ethel Sue said he and her mother were making it for a while last year. Ethel—"

"Ethel Sue Shufflet is trash!" Selma Rillbon slammed the knife on the counter. "Godless sinful trash."

"She's my friend."

"Listen to your mother, girl!" Pat Rillbon took a wedge of pie from his wife, put the plate in front of Angus.

"Ethel Sue knows what's going on, Daddy." Peaches turned the plate her mother put before her around, the point of the pie away from her, and began to eat the crust. "You ought to hire me on, Angus. I hear a lot when I'm helping out up there at the Lyneses. I mean, what they talk about when they think nobody's listening. And what they do when they think nobody's looking."

"Angus doesn't want to hear any gossip from you," Pat said.

"It's not gossip. It's the truth. You ask Jeff. He can tell you, too. Like about Bobby Horewood and Mr. Cumberley's ex-wife. Bet you didn't know that, did you, Angus?"

"Be quiet, girl!" Pat Rillbon's voice was angry.

"Bobby Horewood is wicked and evil," Selma said. "You just eat your pie and be quiet."

"But, Mama, it's the truth. And you saw what she did to me yesterday. She and that Mark Nailles—"

"PEACHES!"

"Oh, all right, Daddy." Peaches cut her eyes to Angus. She knew that she had made her point with him.

When the meal was over Angus pushed his chair back and rose. "I appreciate your asking me, Mrs. Rillbon. But I've got to get going." To Pat Rillbon he said, "If you see Bobby Horewood, you tell him I'm looking for him. I want to know what he did with those gaffs he had Friday night." Mrs. Rillbon and Peaches were collecting the dishes.

"You ask him about that Mrs. Cumberley, you hear?" Peaches said quickly, then looked at her mother when Selma Rillbon put the dishes down with a clatter.

Pat walked to the door with Angus and watched him as he got into his patrol car and drove off.

On his way to Mount Tabor Church, Angus thought about Bobby Horewood. They had gone through high school together but had never been good friends. Where Angus was quiet Bobby was brash. The girls thought he was the best-looking man in the county. So did Bobby. He flashed his bold good looks like a free pass through anybody's gate; he made no secret of the sexual appeal of his vigorous body which he emphasized with tight jeans and heavy gold chains and the extravagant gold ID bracelet he wore. His dark good looks were overlaid with an aura of danger that was as enticing to women as it was foreboding.

Nobody knew much about where he had come from. He had lived alone in a small stone house near View Halloo Farm since he was in high school; before that he had lived with a couple in the western part of the county, but they were not his parents. Bobby had told Angus once that he didn't know who his parents were, that he had been left with his foster family when he was a small boy. He told Angus that the heavy gold bracelet was a present from the man Solverson who lived at View Halloo Farm.

Bobby had taken him there once when they were seniors to swim in the big pool. Solverson, a man in his forties, was in the pool and had come into the dressing room while they were changing. Bobby seemed to flaunt his robust nakedness before them and the man had put an arm familiarly around Bobby's shoulders while he chatted easily with them. Angus's uneasiness had turned to panic when the man suggested that the three of them might like to "have a little fun."

Angus had pulled his trousers on, picked up the rest of his clothes, and finished dressing outside by the pool. He was waiting at Bobby's four-year-old Camaro convertible when the two of them came out of the dressing room ten minutes later. Angus ignored the man's soft apology as he got into the car beside Bobby.

"Jesus, Bobby, you let him do things to you?" he had asked on his way back to town.

Bobby laughed. "It doesn't do any harm. He's always good for something, like a nice watch. Play it right, you can get yourself a car like mine."

Bobby Horewood still lived in the little stone house. Angus wondered what game he was playing now with Amy Cumberley. And anybody else.

CHAPTER 21

Angus called the sheriff at the office but learned little from him. Skinker had drawn a blank when he went to Sweet Valley to find Brod Nailles and he and the sheriff were now in the sheriff's office trying to figure out who at the commune they could charge with obstructing justice. Angus was not surprised at Skinker's failure.

At Mount Tabor Church he sat in his patrol car and watched the mourners gather while he read through his notebook. He added a tentative note or two to his timetable while he waited. Irby Jepson's hearse was pulled up near the front steps and Irby in a black suit was standing at the doorway greeting the mourners.

Angus knew the routine. Irby would ask them to sign the guest register in the vestibule; they'd file in and take their seats not too far forward to appear pushy and not too far back to appear distant and uncaring. Some of them would walk to the front of the church and peer down at old Mrs. Anderson, her white hair now crimped in waves she would have never tolerated in life, her cold hands crossed over her dark blue dress. Everybody would say don't she look natural while thinking she never looked like that while she was breathing. Women would lean forward and tap friends on a shoulder, murmuring platitudes. Men in unaccustomed suits would shake hands with other men and sit stock still, staring ahead and wondering if there'd be rain before the corn got planted.

They would whisper when members of the family appeared. The whispers most often passed on bits of gossip. Angus had heard them at other funerals.

At Mark Nailles's funeral there would be plenty of that, but nobody could say he looked natural. Irby could do a good job on

Jack Lynes given the chance, but it would take work to make anything natural out of Mark Nailles.

All of them would be there: the Barrells, looking proper and wishing they were somewhere else; the Mathers, if they were speaking to each other; the Foster Gloves. Mrs. Cumberley. Mr. Cumberley would not be there, even though these were his friends, or former friends.

What could a preacher say about Mark Nailles inside a church? That he got young girls pregnant and—how would a preacher describe what Annabel had shown him? That he had raped a young black girl and in college had burned a woman with cigarettes in terrible places? That on the night he was killed he was discovered behind the barn with a seventeen-year-old whose father threatened him? That the girl's mother was the one who had been burned? Oh my. Don't he look natural.

What would they whisper at Jack Lynes's funeral? "They say he was trying to make it with the teenager who lived on his farm, the same one as the other one who was killed." "Wasn't he mixed up in that business about Selma, years ago?" "That's Nailles's widow over there. She wouldn't divorce him, but she's been sleeping with Nick Mathers. That's him over there. That's his wife over there on the other side. The one next to her is Amy Cumberley, she was shacking up with Mark Nailles, only she was also getting it off with a young fellow, Bobby Horewood. She was married to Cap Cumberley. He's the one the judge appointed to be commonwealth's attorney when his father died." "Oh yes. Drinks, I heard." "Not anymore." "He sure looked like he had the other day." "Lost his law business; then his daughter died from an abortion. That's what they say." "He's not clean in this business. He was seen at Lynes's barn that night." "Remember old Fess Lynes? Built Copperfields before the First World War. Was some trouble with women there, once, but they hushed it up." "Like they hushed up that trouble with Jack at the University. It's the way they do, they hush things up. This will be hushed up too, mark my words.

"That's Pat Rillbon and his wife Selma. She's the one, you remember. That business at the University. She's a cold one but you never know. That daughter of theirs gets it from somewhere.

"That black woman sitting with the family? She cooks for them. Got a daughter lives in New York City. It was hushed up, but they say her daddy was some friend of the Lyneses, he slipped under the sheets.

"Now you mention it, there's something about her eyes and nose does bear a resemblance. To that one over there."

Angus was in the rear of the church, standing up to see which one it was who looked like Serene Allan. Of course! It's that one. That one!

He awoke, startled, and sat up. Pallbearers were coming out of the church with old Mrs. Anderson. He started his engine, turned on his flashing signal, holding the image of Serene's brother in his mind. It was so clear to him; how had he missed seeing it before?

When the cortege was organized he pulled out in front of the procession. At the intersection with the main highway he stood in the middle of the pavement holding oncoming traffic while the mourners turned right and headed toward the cemetery. Traffic coming from the opposite direction slowed when the drivers saw the red flashing light and picked up speed as soon as they saw it was a funeral.

One of the last of the mourners was turning when a car came up to the intersection, slowed, and turned left into the road to Mount Tabor. As the car passed behind him Angus saw that the driver was Selma Rillbon. She looked up from her driving and caught his eye. The earnest concentration in her face changed to astonishment and then to confusion as she passed and went away from him.

CHAPTER 22

When the last car was on its way Angus took the road back to Mount Tabor and turned north to View Halloo Farm. The house where Bobby Horewood lived stood beside a woods opposite the entrance to the estate. Bobby told people that Mr. Solverson let him live in the small house while he worked at View Halloo and went to high school. When he finished high school and went to work for Buck Bolton he stayed on.

A hundred yards beyond and opposite the elaborate entrance to Solverson's place a worn dirt track led up the hill beside heavy woods to a clearing where Bobby's stone cottage stood. It had been there for more than a hundred years and had a primitive look that was not improved by Bobby's tenancy. As Angus turned into the track he saw that there was an automobile stopped beside the small porch. It was not Bobby's. It was the one that Selma Rillbon had been driving.

Angus backed out and turned around. There was no screen at the foot of the hill where he could park and wait or watch without being seen. At the white gates to View Halloo he turned around and drove past the dirt track. A hundred yards beyond, the road curved around the hill. In the shelter of the uphill bank he could park and watch the entrance to the dirt road without being seen from the house.

He looked at his watch. He should have been back at the office half an hour earlier; his relief would be waiting. But he wanted to stay there until Mrs. Rillbon came down the hill.

While he waited he tried to put things together. Bobby Horewood and Pat Rillbon both had access to the steel cockspurs. Rillbon said some of them were missing. Both of them had had the opportunity to kill Mark Nailles and either of them could have killed Jack Lynes. Pat Rillbon had motives, even though he apparently did not know that Peaches had met Nailles behind the barn. If what Peaches had said about Bobby Horewood and Amy Cumberley were true, there could have been trouble between Bobby and Nailles. But there was no reason for Bobby to kill Jack Lynes. Unless Jack Lynes knew something about Nailles's murder.

Almost every one at Copperfields had left the fights at one time or another during the night to go outside, but the timetable was still incomplete.

Now the latest question was what Selma Rillbon knew, and what she was doing at Bobby's house. Did she suspect her husband and was looking for Bobby because of the spurs? She was the only one he could rule out being involved with Bobby. Amy Cumberley, yes, but Mrs. Rillbon? She had called him wicked and evil.

A flash of sun against metal brought his attention back to the moment. Selma Rillbon's car was coming down the hill. Angus waited until she reached the road, turned south, and drove away from him. Then he drove up the hill.

Angus walked around the house. It was scarcely larger than a garage, built of sturdy stone with a brick chimney at one side and a wooden shed room at the rear. The only sign of modern improvement was an electric meter against the chimney. On the small open porch at the back door an enameled pan hung on a nail above a small shelf. On the shelf was a plastic dish with a bar of soap, and water trickled in a small stream from a faucet below the shelf.

The door pushed easily inward. The room contained a small electric stove, a refrigerator, a table, and two chairs. Open shelves over the stove held boxes and cans of foodstuff and some cooking utensils. A small sink with a wooden drainboard in a corner held a rack of dishes. Angus was astonished at how clean and neat the room was.

A low door through the heavy stone wall led to the front room. The rough plaster walls had been painted white. There was a narrow bed in a corner, a tall chest next to it, a battered sofa near the chimney, and an iron heating stove on the hearth. The front door was blocked by a table and chair and the window next to the door was curtained with a piece of heavy canvas. The wall above the bed was unbroken by windows but was filled with pictures. Dozens of them, unframed, fastened with tape and tacks. The seductive centerfolds from *Playboy* magazine kept company with the bawdier, more explicit nudity of *Penthouse* and *Hustler.* Soft nymphs with half-closed eyes and half-opened thighs shared the space with rammish men from *Playgirl,* flaunting their tumid toys and their California tans, and with photographs of men, women, and men and women in calisthenics that would have made a Pompeiian mosaic-layer blush. What had Selma Rillbon thought when she saw them?

Angus knew that without a warrant he was jeopardizing any evidence he might find, but he did not know what he was looking for, anyway. Something to tell him why Selma Rillbon had been there, something to lead him to the missing cockspurs, something to explain what it was about Bobby Horewood that gave him a sense of uneasiness.

He opened the drawers of the chest one by one. The only clothes in the drawer were a few T-shirts and briefs, some faded jeans, socks, shirts. In the bottom drawer some blankets folded neatly away. Like the other things in the house, the clothes were neatly arranged. A Whitman's candy box in the top drawer was filled with gold and silver jewlery: Chains, medallions, heavy gold rings, two gold watches, some heavy gold link bracelets. They were real and they were valuable. Angus remembered what Bobby had said to him that day at Solverson's and decided that Bobby might not have come by them honorably, but he had not stolen them. Something of value had been exchanged.

Under the blankets he found a handful of paperback books filled with photographs even more "sexplicit" than those on the walls. Three men in sailor hats disported themselves through acrobatic postures of singular variety; two women and a man dallied (without the hats) at the same games and at others denied the sailors. Two men and a woman pursued the same and other frolics. Everything that Angus had ever heard of and things that had never occurred to him were memorialized in those pages.

He brought himself up with a start when he realized that he wasn't paying proper attention. Bobby Horewood could surprise him at any moment.

He put the books back after a last glance and went on to the table against the door. There was nothing of interest on the table; some magazines and a J. C. Penney catalog. He pulled open the shallow drawer in the apron of the table. Several cheap ballpoint pens, some paper, and envelopes. In a far corner of the drawer he found a heavy envelope of cream paper bulging from something solid inside. He lifted the flap and pulled out the heavy card and a small stack of photographs. A bold backhand scrawl in black ink said, "Thanks for the real thing!" The photographs were instant camera shots in color, and they were all of Bobby Horewood.

Except for the lack of polished photographic skill, they were much like the pictures on the wall. Bobby lounging against a cushion, his naked body tan and glowing; Bobby standing against a window, his muscles highlighted in the sunlight; Bobby in a shower, soaking wet, his youthful mettle proud. There was a hircine lechery in the pictures that was missing in those on the walls, despite all the skills of the magazine photographers. Bobby's ease seemed to say this is the way it ought to be. Free and natural.

It was the background that interested Angus. The cushions were soft and luxurious, the curtains at the window expensive, the tiles in the shower costly and elegant. Behind the cushions of the lounge in one picture were a lamp and table; there were several photographs in silver frames on the table. Angus took the pictures to the window, pulled back the canvas, and examined them carefully but he could not make out who the people were in the tiny frames. He only knew that the pictures had been taken in a woman's room. He slid the card back in the envelope, replaced it in its corner, and closed the drawer with a feeling of relief.

Handling the pictures had almost been like handling Bobby himself. The pictures on the wall had turned him off, like seeing too much food spread out at once, but the pictures of Bobby had stirred something dark and troubling in him, a sudden apprehensive fear of something unrecognized, some dark music from the shadowy woods.

Nowhere in the room did he find the missing cockspurs, or any indication that Bobby Horewood had a connection with

Nailles. He went out through the kitchen and pulled the door shut behind him. He was glad to be outside in the afternoon light, away from the shadows of the adjacent woods. He drove back to Phoebeville faster than was necessary.

What struck him most forcibly about Bobby's house was that, although Bobby had lived there for more than five years, there was no sense of permanence there. Bobby was a transient, stopping off only as long as it suited him.

CHAPTER 23

The sheriff and Vern Wishburn, Angus's relief, were in the office when he arrived.

"Where the hell have you been?" Rowe demanded. "I didn't authorize no overtime for you."

"I was following up on something, Sheriff."

"You follow up what I tell you to follow up, we'd have this thing wrapped up. As it is that boy's got clean away. I been sitting here at the telephone all afternoon trying to get the word out in other counties to be on the lookout for him. If you'd done what I told you to yesterday, Jack Lynes would still be alive."

"I don't think so, sir. Nailles's son didn't kill those two men."

"Then who the hell did, Mr. Sherlock Holmes?"

"Can I talk to you alone, Sheriff?" Angus knew that Wishburn told everything he heard or did to his wife. People said she had opened her beauty shop so she could gossip. Wishburn at a gesture from the sheriff picked up his hat and went out the door.

"All right, Bealle. What's so big you can't talk in front of another law enforcement officer?"

"You know how Mrs. Wishburn talks."

"She's a bigmouth, that's for sure."

"I don't think we can make a case against Nailles's son just because of that fight they had."

"What about that stuff that woman told you? And he was at Copperfields Friday night. Told you so himself."

"But he didn't have any reason to kill Jack Lynes."

"If Jack Lynes caught on that he had killed his old man, that's reason enough."

"But Lynes didn't think Brod Nailles did it. You heard what those two others said. About not doing it to the boy."

"Well then, who the hell did it?"

"Somebody else already had good reasons."

"Who?"

"Pat Rillbon for one. You told me yourself what Nailles and Lynes did to Mrs. Rillbon. Even though it's hard to see him killing them, he has the best motives, the best opportunity, and the best chance to get at the weapons."

"Rillbon's been living there all these years without killing anybody. Why would he do something like that now?"

"Peaches. She told me she met Mark Nailles outside and went around behind the barn with him. That was near the end of the fights, after Pat Rillbon caught him talking to her and gave him hell about it. Peaches said somebody saw her and Nailles there. Brod Nailles heard Pat threaten Nailles when he told him to stay away from Peaches. And Pat Rillbon told me that Jack Lynes has been giving Peaches money and presents. Rillbon has the key to the box where the gaffs are kept, and there are a couple of sets missing. One of them is the kind they call slashers."

"Yeah. I know about slashers. They don't use them around here."

"Pat Rillbon could have used them to kill Jack Lynes. As drunk as Lynes was Saturday night, anybody could have cut his throat without a fight."

"The boy could have stole them spurs. It just ain't like Pat Rillbon to do a thing like that."

"I know. But who else is there?"

The sheriff shifted uneasily in his chair. "You think you can make it stick?"

"I think we ought to see if we can find those slashers. Nobody looked for the weapon this morning."

"Those folks at Copperfields ain't going to stay there forever, if they ain't gone already. I don't care who did it. I just want to get this thing off my back and I ain't going to spend the taxpayers' money on no wild-goose chases. You go over and talk to Cumberley, see what he thinks. If he says we got some kind of a case, you go out to Copperfields and take a look around, then bring Rillbon in so we can question him here. But you be sure you're right about him, you understand? I'm not going to get my ass hung up if you mess it up."

"Yes, sir."

From the bright weather of the morning, the day was changing. When Angus left the office, clouds had gathered over the mountains to the west and the maples in the courthouse lawn were whipping in a brisk breeze. The temperature had dropped and the air was turning cold. He walked across the courthouse lawn, stood in front of the commonwealth's attorney's office for several minutes, tried the knob of the door and found it locked, then turned and went back to his car.

Buck Bolton's Exxon station was closed on Sundays, but the door to the garage was up and someone was moving about inside. Angus recognized Bobby Horewood's souped-up Camaro convertible pulled up beside the grease pit. Bobby had the hood up and was bending over the engine when Angus stopped his patrol car at the pumps and got out. Bobby looked up and nodded but continued fussing with the distributor wires, whistling softly.

"You got a minute, Bobby?"

Bobby Horewood wiped his hands on a rag and turned around, pulled the hood down and closed it. His dark eyes under his thick lashes were challenging without being insolent. Angus, remembering the photographs in the drawer, felt again in Bobby's smiling animation something apprehensive, remembered the virile nakedness. As though he had read Angus's mind, Bobby hitched his crotch and leaned against the Camaro. He did not stop whistling.

"You handled some roosters for Jack Lynes Friday night." Angus had to clear his throat to get rid of the hoarseness and to cover the flush that came over him.

"Might as well have been hens, all the fight they had. Pat doesn't take care of his birds like he ought to."

"Pat Rillbon said he left the cupboard in the office open for you to use the spurs. Doctor Panthorpe found one in Nailles's body and Rillbon says some of his are missing."

"You accusing me of cutting up that man, Angus?" Horewood came around the side of the Camaro to the driver's door, his eyes on Angus as he moved.

"I'm not accusing anybody. I'm just trying to find out where the gaff came from and who put it in Nailles's body."

"It didn't come from me. I still got the ones I used." He walked around the front of the Camaro, opened the passenger door, and leaned in, rummaging in the glove compartment. He searched briefly but confidently, then his movements became quicker, and finally he began pulling things from the compartment and throwing them on the seat. Angus went around the car to look over Bobby's shoulder as he searched. Bobby emptied the compartment, then turned around smiling. He held out a small leather case, then looked at it and his smile disappeared.

"There ain't but one gaff in here."

Angus took the case from him. The way Bobby had handled it, there was no need to protect it for fingerprints now. "When was it you last saw them?"

"I had them in here Friday night. I swear to God, Angus. I got a witness to that."

"You're sure you put both of them in here?"

"Pat didn't have but three cocks to fight. After they was over, I kept hold of them."

"Why didn't you put them back in the cupboard?"

Bobby's dark eyes sparkled. "There was other things I was doing. I didn't get to it."

"You kept them with you all night?"

"I was wearing them clipped on my belt like they was meant to be worn."

"When did you put them in your car?"

"About the time everything was over. Before midnight, I'd say."

"You still live out at Solverson's place? View Halloo?"

"You know I do, Angus."

"Do you still go over there? Like when we were in school?"

"Sometimes. Solverson likes them in high school better."

"Did that man Barrell ever try anything with you?"

Bobby flashed Angus a hard look. "That's got nothing to do with who killed those two guys."

"He was in your car with you Friday night."

"We were just getting a drink out of my bottle."

"What time was that?"

"Around eleven, maybe. How'd you find out about that?"

"Somebody saw you. He try anything?"

Bobby shrugged. "Sure, he tried. He was at the station here Friday afternoon. Told me Solverson was a friend of his, said we ought to get to know each other. He wanted to meet me somewhere after everything was over Friday night. I told him I had something else going."

"Mrs. Cumberley?"

Bobby ran his hand through his curls and smiled. "Jesus. There ain't nothing a secret anymore. You trying to get me into trouble, Angus?"

"Not unless you're already in trouble."

"How'd you find out about me and her?"

"It's true, then?"

"Hey, man, that one's a real fireball. I'd had to fight her off with a stick, if I'd wanted to fight her off. She came by the station half a dozen times the last two weeks buying gas, when she didn't need but a gallon or so at a time. How the hell did you find out about her and me?" Angus did not answer and when the silence got long enough Bobby went on. "I've been going out there in the evenings to help Pat Rillbon try to get those cocks of his in shape for the fights. You know, feed them dog food and dried blood to make them look good and shiny and exercise them. Pat never paid no attention to them; he just let them run in the yards. I'd take them over to the barn, put them little leather boots over the spurs, and let them fight some. I'd throw the birds up in the air, let them land on this foam rubber pad to make their wings strong. She'd come down to the barn while I was there."

"How'd she know you were there?"

Horewood grinned. "Oh hell, Angus, I told her at the station I'd be there. She was all over me, and all over that foam rubber. Chicken feathers and all." He grinned and licked his lips remembering. "I know damn well she didn't tell you."

Angus shook his head. "No. She didn't tell me."

"Then it must have been Jeff. He caught us at it one night. Didn't seem to bother her much. But don't you think it had anything to do with killing those two men. All it was was another roll on the pad." He laughed.

"Didn't you know she was Mark Nailles's girlfriend?"

"I did when I saw them Friday night. I asked Barrell about it, he said they'd been at it for about a year. But I noticed they didn't get on too well that night. She was mad as hell about something." Horewood raised his T-shirt and scratched his taut hairy belly. "He was a mean-looking bastard. He had it in mind making it with Peaches that night, but he was spitting in the wrong well there."

"You saw them together?"

"They took off around that shed, but they didn't stay too long. Not long enough."

"Was that while you were in your car with Barrell?"

"It was while I was somewhere outside. When the fights were about over. My car was parked around by the shed."

"While you were there did you see anybody else around the shed?"

"There were people coming and going; I didn't pay much attention."

"You don't remember anybody but Nailles and Peaches?"

"Well, there was Nailles's girlfriend, Cumberley. She was looking for him. And her ex, who lives here in Phoebeville."

"You saw him there?"

"He was stumbling around out there in the dark."

"How do you mean, stumbling?"

"Drunk, man. Like he was drunk. He went around the shed where Peaches and that other one had gone; then he came back and got in his car, and pretty soon they came around from there. Then they heard somebody coming around the barn, and Nailles ducks into the shed."

"Where did Peaches go?"

"Peaches? She cut out in the dark around the corner of the shed."

"Did you see who it was—the other person?"

"I told you, man, it was her—the Cumberley woman. She hollered his name a couple of times then she went back the way she came. I went back in the barn to see if the fights was ending up."

"What time did all this happen?"

"Hey, I didn't look at no watches. The fights went on till about midnight. It was before that. Maybe eleven-thirty or -forty. I don't know, man."

"Did you stay inside until they were over?"

"Barrell wanted to mess around in the car, but I told him I'd meet him later, where the tractor shed was. He was waiting for me when I went around there when the fights was ending. We hadn't been there five minutes when somebody came in the door. He said, 'Mark? That you, Mark?' Sloppy, like he was drunk. When Barrell heard him he crawled around behind the tractor. I heard the man say, 'Oh Jesus!' or something like that when he saw what was going on and he turned around and went out. Barrell was scared out of his head. He crawled behind the tractor in one hell of a hurry."

"What did you do?"

"Pulled up my pants and went back to my car." He stiffened suddenly and snapped his fingers. "Hey! Maybe that's where I lost my knife!"

"What knife?"

"My sheath knife I've had since I was twelve. Had it on my belt, but when I got home it was gone. I figured it fell off when— when we was there. No way was I going back to look for it when I heard what happened."

"There wasn't any knife there when Nailles was found. I searched the shed myself. Doctor Panthorpe found the gaff in Nailles."

"Then I must have dropped it somewhere else."

Angus felt his heart beating fast. "What did Barrell do?"

"I didn't see Barrell again. He said he was going to make it worth my while. He still owes me."

"Christ sake! Isn't there anything you won't do for money?"

"Not money, Angus. He was going to put me onto a job. I'm getting out of this dead-ass place."

"You know what time that was?"

"It was after I saw Nailles and Peaches. Maybe ten minutes."

"About eleven forty-five?"

"That, I'd say."

"Did you know that Barrell was Nailles's brother-in-law?"

"We didn't get around to who his kin was. That wasn't on his mind at the time."

Angus shook his head. "Why'd you do a thing like that?"

Bobby grinned goatishly. "I'm doing them a favor, they'll do me a favor back." He shrugged. "You'd be surprised the offers I get. Maybe it's because I'm thinking about it all the time. I wake up in the morning, all day long pumping gas and changing oil I think about making it with who comes in there. And I can tell you, they're thinking about making it with me, too. Every night I'm off somewhere making it with somebody who just can't wait. Sometimes in the afternoon, too. You think it's some kind of gift I've got, Angus?"

Angus said he didn't know.

"That Mrs. Cumberley called me a satyr. That's some kind of half-man half-goat she said lived a long time ago. They went around screwing all the time and making people want it. She also said I was like some god called Pan these satyrs worshipped."

"It was the Greeks and Romans believed that."

"If them satyrs had sisters, she must be one of them. You know how it is with older women, Angus. The young ones got the fire, but the older ones—well, you know."

"Doesn't it mean anything more to you than just a quick poke?"

"You ever see a bull or a stallion? You think it means anything more to them?"

"But you're not an animal. You're a man."

"Hey, man, we're all animals. How do you think I graduated from high school? I passed social studies because old Miss Teasesley was getting it off with me once a week."

"She was fifty years old, for God's sake!"

"She wasn't too old to want it. Still does, every time she buys gas. And Coach Bonn who taught chemistry? Gave me a B in his class. He thought it was fair exchange."

Angus dropped the subject. "You sure you put those gaffs here in the compartment?"

"I told you, man. When I got the whiskey out, I had them clipped on my belt. I put them in there when I was leaving. I didn't know there was one of them missing." Horewood walked around his car, opened the door, and slipped into the driver's seat. "Somebody stole my whiskey. They could have got them spurs, too."

"When was it you found that out?"

"Wasn't until sometime yesterday. When I was looking for my sheath knife. I didn't look for the whiskey when I tossed the spurs in."

"There's something else. What would Mrs. Rillbon be doing at your house?"

Bobby struck the sides of his head with the palms of his hands in mock desperation. "I tell you, man, I don't know what it is about me."

"I don't believe that. Not Mrs. Rillbon."

"Believe it, fellow. Look, I got to roll. I promised the farm manager up at Solverson's I'd help him with some sheep this afternoon." He started the Camaro with a roar. He grinned at Angus as he backed out of the garage. "Don't worry about the sheep. You got to draw the line somewhere." Halfway to the street he stopped, drove forward to where Angus was standing. "You go up there to Copperfields and figure out which one of those dudes took my whiskey and my knife and gaff, and I'll come up and show you who it was killed those muh-fuhs." Without waiting for Angus to answer him, he backed into the street and gunned off out of Phoebeville.

CHAPTER 24

Cap Cumberley's old-fashioned redbrick house on the edge of Phoebeville stood well back from the street. The grass needed cutting, and there were pickets missing from the front fence. The rising turbulence of the afternoon thrashed the fresh leaves of the old maples on the lawn. A wooden swing on the wide porch banged against the railing and the green chairs bobbed on their rockers; bits of wisteria blossoms from the overgrown vine along the roofline blew across the porch as Angus rang the doorbell.

Cumberley took him through a dark hall into a littered sitting room, pushed papers from a chair, and asked Angus to sit. He had not shaved and he wore the same shirt and trousers he had worn Saturday afternoon. He looked worn and tired, and Angus smelled the sourness of whiskey on his breath.

"You heard about Mr. Lynes?"

Cumberley said he had.

Angus told him about the gaff Panthorpe had found in Nailles's body and what Bobby Horewood had told him about the gaffs and his knife. "The sheriff wanted to arrest Nailles's son. I found him out at Sweet Valley last night, but he's not there now."

"What evidence have you got?"

"Brod Nailles went looking for his father. He was at the barn Friday night. He was fired up about—about something he had learned." Angus's throat was dry, and he swallowed hard. "It had to do with a fight they had last year. Something to do with a —a girl."

"I heard about the fight, but I never knew what brought it on."

Angus did not want to discuss with Cumberley what Annabel had told him. He knew that he could never say it. "Maybe he had a reason to kill his father, but there's no reason why he should kill Mr. Lynes."

"Unless Jack Lynes somehow knew what he had done."

"Lynes was drinking heavily all night and was bothered about something. Mathers said that last night Lynes kept saying something about not doing it to the boy. Maybe he thought we were going to arrest Brod Nailles. But we don't know that Brod was there last night."

"We don't know he wasn't, do we?"

"No, sir. But he was at Sweet Valley most of the evening. But there's somebody else."

Cumberley looked at him steadily. "Pat Rillbon."

"Yes, sir. Brod Nailles heard him arguing with Nailles outside the barn Friday night. Rillbon told him to keep away from Peaches." Angus rotated the brim of his hat nervously in his hands. He had reached the moment he had been dreading. "You must have heard it, Mr. Cumberley."

Cumberley did not take his eyes from Angus. "No, Angus. I didn't hear it. I was too far away." Angus said nothing, and he went on. "I wondered when you would know I was there. I know the sheriff's attitude about cockfighting and I know the general public feeling about it around here. So after supper Friday I was sitting here alone, and I decided to drive out to Copperfields and see what was going on, who was there. It wasn't a wise thing to do. After all, I am the chief law enforcement officer in the county, even if I do have discretion in prosecuting misdemeanors like gambling and cockfighting. I didn't go inside the barn, but I did go to the door and look in. Pat Rillbon saw me as he was going in. I didn't know where he had been or that he had been arguing with Nailles. I looked inside for a few minutes, saw who was in the crowd, then went back to where I was parked. I didn't see Nailles or Jack Lynes inside but I saw Amy and Fossy Glove. I thought maybe Rillbon would break up the fights if he thought I was going to make a case of it, so I went back to my car." Cumberley rubbed his forehead with his fingers, pressing the temples as if his long speech had tired him.

"What time was that?"

"Must have been ten-thirty, maybe. When I got there."

"Did anybody else see you?"

"I don't know. Later on two men were tapping a bottle in a car near mine. One of them got out and went back to the barn. It was that young man at the Exxon station, Bobby. I forget his last name."

"Horewood. Who was the other man?"

"I didn't pay much attention. I sat there for a while; I stayed in my car because I didn't want—Amy to see me. What else have you got that points to Pat Rillbon?"

"Brod Nailles heard them arguing and there was a scuffle. And he saw Rillbon taking Peaches away. Nailles threatened to go to Jack Lynes and have Rillbon fired. Rillbon says that Jack Lynes has been giving Peaches money and presents. It's tearing him apart, Mr. Cumberley, knowing the way Peaches is. And after all that business years ago with Mrs. Rillbon—"

"You think that's enough of a motive?"

"It could be, if it was all building up inside. And he had the key to the cockspurs. He could get to them *any time.*"

"What about the knife?"

"I don't know if that's the weapon."

"So you want to charge him with murder?"

"Not if he didn't do it."

"You want me to tell you you've got a case?"

"It doesn't seem fair. All his life Mr. Rillbon has done what he had to do. He's a good man. Nailles was a rotten bastard and except for his money Jack Lynes doesn't seem to turn out much more than a drunk. The others up there—Mathers and Barrell and Glove, and their wives—the way they are in the sack with other people—" Angus stopped.

"Never mind, Angus, I know what you're getting at. Go on with what you were saying."

"What I mean is, I may have to arrest a good man for murdering a couple of rotten ones."

"You're a policeman, Angus. You can't base a case on whether you like somebody. I like Rillbon, too, but I'll have to prosecute him if you bring me the evidence."

"He's the only one who would have a reason to kill Lynes if Nailles did what he threatened to do."

"I don't think Jack Lynes would have taken any such threat

seriously. Pat Rillbon is too good to lose, and Jack Lynes knew what Nailles was like. If he knew Rillbon killed Nailles, he would be concerned about Brod, wouldn't he?"

"The sheriff wants me to bring Rillbon in for questioning."

"You've eliminated all the others? That is, if you assume that someone at Copperfields did it?"

"Well, Mathers wasn't there—"

"Can he prove that?"

"He says he has a witness."

"Have you checked him?"

"It was her. No, sir."

"Of course. It would be her, not him."

"Glove doesn't have any apparent motive, and Barrell—"

"You think he's too—soft—to murder somebody?"

"You remember I told you about Serene Allan—how some friend of Lynes's father seduced her mother?"

"Good lord! You think it was Barrell's father who did it?"

"I hit on it earlier today, the resemblance. If Nailles and Lynes knew about that—you think that could be a motive?"

"Nailles might not know, but I'm sure Jack Lynes knew. It all happened in his parents' house. Barrell is a snob. Such a thing getting out might hurt his pride, but it wouldn't make him kill. Aristocratic Southern blood flows in a lot of black veins. Something like that wouldn't drive him to kill."

"Yes, sir."

"Nailles didn't like him. It's Sally Carter's money the Barrells live on mostly. That's his best reason not to kill a brother-in-law who makes the family money. You get enough on Rillbon to take it to a grand jury, you'll be okay. But you just be sure before you move."

"What I've got to do is find out who got hold of those spurs, or that knife." He told Cumberley what Bobby Horewood had said. That Bobby had put the spurs in his car, but whoever took his whiskey might have taken the gaff, too.

"Maybe somebody was desperate for a drink." Cumberley rubbed his unshaven chin. "I know something about that."

"Yes, sir. What about the gaff?"

"Get that spur from Horewood to Rillbon. You establish that, you might have a case."

"But Lynes, his throat was cut with a sharp blade."

"Then you'll have to tie that to him, too. With the knife?"

Angus felt his body go clammy remembering the sight. He took the ignominious memory with him to his car, seeing the soiled ivy at the base of the terrace. The dark clouds had turned to gusty winds and the rain was blowing against the glass of his patrol car when Angus ran toward it. The gray purple sky had blown out of the west to darken the afternoon. Angus got his rain gear from the trunk and put it on. His stomach turned over again as he sat behind the wheel, this time with the chill of excitement. Something had come back to him. That morning, with his head hanging over the balustrade, there was something he had not taken in. He had been too busy throwing up. But he remembered now.

CHAPTER 25

On the way to Copperfields a branch blew across the road ahead of him, and he stopped to pull it off the paved way. At the gate to Copperfields a downed power line arced on the wet ground.

There was a new white Chrysler convertible in the drive in front of the main house. Three people at the open front door turned to look as Angus drove up. He recognized Mrs. Barrell but did not know the woman in the dark dress with her. The third person was Brod Nailles. He wore a shirt and tie and blue jacket and chinos.

As Angus stepped out of his patrol car Brod Nailles hesitated for a moment then ran down the steps and across the grass away from the house. The woman with Mrs. Barrell called out for him to wait, but Brod kept going. Angus ran down the drive after him, saw him turn in at the road leading to the barn. Angus's heavy rain gear made it difficult for him to run, and he knew that he could not catch Brod. He ran back to his patrol car and whipped it around the drive and into the road. Brod was still running. The rain had soaked his jacket and water splashed from his feet. As Angus caught up with him he looked over his shoulder, turned and ran toward the fence bordering the road, vaulted it nimbly, and went off across the field toward the barn.

Angus saw the red flashing lights of the sheriff's car coming up the lane from the highway as he got out of his car at the barn. He watched as Rowe skidded into the side road and drove up to the barn, throwing water and wet grass as he plowed to a stop.

"What the hell you doing, letting him get away?" Rowe shouted as he crabbed his way out of his car. "You ain't worth a good goddamn, Bealle."

"How did you know he was here?"

"Somebody tipped us off. You go around that way, see if you

can find him. Check that shed." As Angus turned, he saw the sheriff take his shotgun out of the trunk of his car. He went back.

"You won't need that, Sheriff."

"We got a killer on our hands, boy." Rowe broke the gun and dropped shells into the breech.

"He's not armed. And we don't know he's a killer."

"He's killer enough for me. You just do like I told you."

"What about Rillbon? That's his pickup parked over there."

"Then one way or another we'll get ourselves a killer." The sheriff walked stiffly toward the barn door, stepping over the orange ribbons that drooped in the storm. Angus saw that the seal on the barn door had not been broken, but let the sheriff go. At the shed door he found the seal intact and went on around the barn. Rain ran down his hat into his face and he wiped it away with a wet hand. There was no way that Brod could get into the barn from the rear; he had to be nearby. Thick plantings of ligustrum and holly grew at the corners of the shed and in front of the barn; Rillbon kept them clipped so that they grew thick at the base. The only place he could hide was in the shrubbery.

Angus moved forward, pushing his way behind the bushes against the wall. Brod was not there. He was headed toward a mass of shrubbery at the opposite corner when the sound of the sheriff's shotgun slammed through the sodden air, followed by a shout. Rowe had left the door to the barn open, but the gray light of the afternoon did nothing to illumine the interior darkness. There was no sound.

"Sheriff? Are you all right?" A dull growl came from the other end of the barn. "Where are you, Sheriff?"

"Bealle! Bealle, goddamn it, get me the hell out of here."

"Where are you?"

"How the hell do I know? I'm over here in the goddamn dark."

Angus found his electric torch in his patrol car and flashed its beam through the barn. Across the cockpit in the smaller room behind it he found the sheriff stretched on the sandy floor. His gun lay four feet away. "Get that damn light out of my eyes."

"What happened?"

"What the hell you think happened? I fell over the damn

bench there. Here, give me a hand. No, not like that. Be careful of my back." He groaned and fell back against the sand. "God-damn gun went off. I could have been killed." He eased himself up on an elbow. "Be careful now."

Angus set the overturned bench up and put his light on it. Rowe screamed and lurched and pushed until Angus had him on his feet, almost doubled up. He left the gun where it was. As he helped the sheriff inch across the cockpit toward the door, he heard the sound of an automobile starting up. At the door he saw that the pickup truck was gone; he ran forward, leaving the sheriff screaming in pain as Angus let go his arm.

"Holy Jesus! boy. Look what you're doing."

When he had Rowe finally in the backseat of his patrol car where he could lie on his back, the sheriff asked, "You find the boy?"

"No, sir."

"It was my gun scared him off. You've screwed this one up good, boy, and I ain't going to forget it. You get me home, then you put out a description of that truck. If it was Rillbon in it, it ain't going far. That boy, I'll bet you he heads straight for Sweet Valley."

"The seal wasn't broken on the door when you went inside."

"What the hell difference does that make?"

"It means that nobody was in the barn." Angus slammed the door and walked around the car. As he opened the door, he saw someone appear at the corner of the shed in a black raincoat and rain hat. The man was halfway to the car before Angus recognized Pat Rillbon.

"I thought I heard a shot. Where's my truck? What's going on?"

"It's the Nailles boy. He went off in your truck."

"That you shooting at him?"

Angus tossed his head toward the backseat. Water from his cap sprayed his hands.

Rillbon peered in at the sheriff. "Jesus. Did he get shot?"

"It's his back." Angus almost laughed. "He fell over a bench and his gun went off. He thought Brod Nailles was in the barn."

A groan from the backseat made Angus turn. "Bealle, you take my car and go after that son of a bitch. Rillbon, you can drive me home. You come back without him it's your ass, you understand?"

"Then you think the boy did it?"

"If it wasn't you, Rillbon. Your nose ain't clean in this."

"You trust a murderer to drive you home?"

"You ain't accused, I just say you ain't cleared, either."

"Whatever you say, Sheriff." Rillbon walked around the car to the driver's side. "As long as I don't have to stand here in the rain."

"And you, Bealle. You find that boy, and you hold him and you charge him. I could have got killed in there, looking for him."

CHAPTER 26

It was still raining when Angus reached the sign at the entrance to Sweet Valley, but not as hard as it had been, and the weather was clearing in the west. There would be no visible sunset but there was promise of a clear night.

He saw the blue pickup as soon as he pulled up at the main house. It was parked beside the shed, its motor still running. Angus backed away, parked his car two hundred feet down the lane against some small pine trees, and walked back to the truck. He found a place out of the rain against a door to the shed and waited.

Driving across the county from Copperfields, Angus had come to two decisions. The first was that he was not going to endure Sheriff Rowe any longer. The state police were always looking for patrolmen and there were other police departments where he would not have to deal with men like Rowe. The second troubled him. He knew that Brod Nailles had not killed his father; neither had Pat Rillbon. Whoever had tipped the sheriff that Brod was at Copperfields knew that the sheriff saw Brod as the principal suspect. But Brod appeared to be just arriving at Copperfields as Angus drove up. The tipster must have known that Brod was on his way and was trying to set him up for the sheriff. What he was going to do was risky and it scared Angus, but he saw no alternative. Sheriff Rowe would shoot Brod on sight.

Angus had stood there for five minutes when he heard someone walking on the gravel. Two figures hurried around the corner of the shed toward the truck. One of them was Annabel, the other was Brod.

He waited until they reached the truck before he stepped forward. Brod had opened the door on the driver's side and turned to say something when he saw Angus. He leaped into the cab, put the truck in gear, and drove forward in a tight circle, almost hitting Annabel as she ran toward the porch of the main house. Mud and grass spun from the wheels as he lurched around and headed down the lane away from the commune.

By the time Angus reached his car and had it turned around in the space between the fences and headed up the lane, the pickup was out of sight beyond a bend in the lane. At the entrance to the graveled road, he saw Brod's tracks in the wet clay. At the paved road he hesitated. If Brod turned right, he was headed back to Copperfields; left he would go south out of the county, unless he turned at the crossroads a mile beyond Sweet Valley. If he turned left there and crossed the river he would reach the highway to Richmond in two miles. That seemed the logical thing for him to do. But Brod was not being logical. The wet road gave him no sign.

Angus whipped his car to the left, headed toward the crossroads. He was still cursing his own stupidity when he reached the crossroads and saw the pickup. It had skidded on the fast turn and slid off the pavement into the drainage ditch. Brod was getting out of the cab as Angus turned at the corner. He stood to face the lights, put his arms up, and waited resignedly for Angus.

He sat shivering in his wet clothes beside Angus as they drove back to Copperfields. "You going to charge me with murder?"

"No. But you stole that pickup. What made you run like that?"

"Because you and that sheriff were going to arrest me. Isn't that so?"

"Why do you think that?"

"Isn't that so?"

"The sheriff wants to, yes. But you didn't have to run."

"He was going to kill me; I heard him shooting inside that barn."

Angus could not deny that. "I know you didn't kill them."

"Who did it, then?"

"How did you know the sheriff was coming after you?"

"What difference does that make? She was just doing me a favor."

"It was a woman? Somebody at the Lynes's?"

"It was Mrs. Lynes."

"How did she know?"

"I don't know. We had just got there. I—" Brod sat up and pulled his wet jacket off, twisting in the seat as he did. Angus turned the heater on. He was warm inside his rain gear, but Brod was shivering. "I went home this morning. To see my mother. She wasn't sorry he's dead, but it wasn't—I don't think she—I thought she ought to have somebody with her. Then when she heard about Mr. Lynes being killed she said she ought to go see Mrs. Lynes. So we drove up here this afternoon. And Aunt Sally, too."

"Aunt Sally?"

"I mean we came up to see her too. My father's sister, Mrs. Barrell. She's a regular pain in the ass but Mother said they had to decide what to do about a funeral. She telephoned Mrs. Lynes before we came and talked to Aunt Sally."

"Then Mrs. Lynes and Mrs. Barrell knew that you were coming. And Mrs. Lynes told you the sheriff was coming after you. So somebody notified him."

"Then it must have been my aunt or uncle. Mrs. Lynes wouldn't have told me if she had called the sheriff." Brod looked quickly at him and then at the floor. "And that's why you were there."

"No, but that's why the sheriff was. He wants this thing wrapped up. He wasn't shooting at you in the barn, but he would have if he'd found you. You didn't have to run off like that, you know."

"You just said he was going to shoot me. The word is out: Pin it on the boy." He had stopped shivering. He shifted in his seat, pulling his damp chinos away from his legs. Angus was beginning to perspire under his rain gear. He rolled a window down. "What are you going to do? Take me to jail?"

"No. I'm taking you back to Copperfields. But first I have to make a telephone call."

At the intersection with Route 59 there was a public telephone outside a small store. He kept an eye on the car as he dialed, but Brod made no sign of bolting.

He let the call ring through ten rings and was about to hang up when Cap Cumberley answered. Angus told him what had happened. Cumberley was silent for so long that Angus called his name. "Oh. Yes, Angus. Yes." He sounded as if he had just been waked up.

"I need your help, Mr. Cumberley. Can you meet me at Copperfields in an hour? Mr. Cumberley? I know it's tough, your wife being there—"

"Yes, Angus." Cumberley cut him off. "Of course. I'll be there. You know what you're doing?"

"Yes, sir. I know what I'm doing." He said it sadly, but with conviction.

CHAPTER 27

On the way to Copperfields he detoured into Phoebeville, left Brod in his car while he walked around the courthouse yard. He had a key to the sheriff's office and knew where the key to Cumberley's office was kept in the sheriff's desk.

Driving to Copperfields he talked to Brod earnestly. Brod listened until Angus had finished. "Holy Jesus! I can't believe it." He was quiet for a minute before he nodded. "You think you can get away with that?"

"If I don't, I'm not staying here anyway."

The Chrysler convertible was still at the doorway. Maggie answered his ring, looked at Brod impassively, and shrugged her shoulders toward the library when Angus asked for Mrs. Lynes.

The library door stood partly open. Angus pushed it tentatively and stood as Kenyon Lynes looked up from the chair next to the fireplace. Mrs. Barrell and the woman who had to be Brod's mother were on the sofa opposite her. Angus saw the distaste in Mrs. Barrell's face as he came in; the other woman looked up.

"Brod. Where's Brod?"

Brod went past Angus to his mother, his wet coat over his arm. "It's okay, Mom."

Kenyon Lynes rose from her chair. "Yes, Officer Bealle. What is it now?"

"He shouldn't have run off like that, Mrs. Lynes. He could have been killed. Why did you tell him we were coming?"

"I'm sorry; I thought he should know."

"I suppose that when you shoot him you'll consider the whole thing closed?" Sally Carter Barrell's voice was sarcastic. "You are going to arrest him now?"

"No, Mrs. Barrell. He didn't do it."

"And I suppose you know who did?"

"I will soon, Mrs. Barrell."

"Please, Sally Carter." Brod's mother turned to her sister-in-law. "There's enough difficulty already."

"There wouldn't be any difficulty at all if the police in this dreary place had any competence." Mrs. Barrell held her hands primly in her lap, but Angus saw that she squeezed her fingers nervously as she talked.

"Don't worry, Aunt Sally. You'll find out soon enough how competent they are." Brod sneezed suddenly and his mother put a hand on his arm.

"You're catching cold, Brod. Your clothes are wet."

Kenyon moved over to him. "Come with me, Brod. I'll get you something dry. They may not fit, but they'll be dry."

Brod looked at Angus for permission. Angus nodded and Brod followed Mrs. Lynes out of the room.

Mrs. Nailles sensed his awkwardness standing there. "You will catch cold, too, standing there in those rain clothes. Why don't you put them in the hall? That is, if you intend to stay."

"Yes, ma'am. I do plan to stay a while." He slipped off his raincoat and took it to the hall, putting it over a chair. When he returned to the library Mrs. Nailles was seated in a chair near the sofa. Mrs. Barrell had not moved. Angus was aware of the deliberate distance between them.

"Can you tell me who is still here?" Angus asked.

Mrs. Barrell looked at him coolly. "Why, everyone, of course. Mr. and Mrs. Glove and the Mathers. My husband, and Mrs. Cumberley. We plan to leave shortly." She looked off into the middle distance away from Angus. "That is, unless you include us among your suspects and intend to hold us here."

"I won't hold anybody I don't have to, Mrs. Barrell."

"I want you to understand, Officer," Mrs. Nailles said, her voice steady. "And you too, Sally Carter. My husband was not a very decent person. He was totally unpleasant. But I want you to do what you have to regardless of who is involved."

Sally Carter Barrell rose from her seat. "You speak as though one of us might be responsible. That's unthinkable."

"There's nothing that's unthinkable anymore."

The door opened. Kenyon Lynes came in, followed by Pat

Rillbon. He spoke to Angus without acknowledging the other women in the room. "I've got the sheriff outside, Angus. Got him almost home and he decided he had to be back here. He had a pint of whiskey in his car, and he's drunk most of it. Says it kills the pain and he's okay."

"A drunken sheriff! That's all we need!" Sally Carter turned in disgust.

"He wants to see you at the car, Angus."

"I'll talk to him later. If you want you can tell him I'm busy right now."

Rillbon's astonishment changed quickly to a small smile at one side of his mouth. "I'll tell him when I leave, Angus. If that's all right."

"You can tell him now, then, Mr. Rillbon. I'd like for you to go and bring Mrs. Rillbon here."

"She's got nothing to do with this." His tone was harsh. He waited for Angus to answer him, and when he saw that there was going to be no answer, said, "I guess she has a right to know what's going on, at any rate. I'll go get her."

"Bring Peaches, too." Rillbon turned and left the room without acknowledging the last instruction. There was a sound of voices in the hall; Angus went to the door and saw that Rillbon had met Cap Cumberley at the front door. Maggie appeared from the back hall in response to Cumberley's ring. Angus felt sweat forming under his arms and running down his sides, but he knew it was not because of the heat.

He took his rain gear and a flashlight and went through the house to the terrace, crossed to the steps, putting his light along the rail. He pushed through the shrubbery on the kitchen side of the steps; the wet leaves brushed against his face, and the rain had washed away the earlier sourness that had clung to his memory. He put his light against the base of the terrace and ran it along the wall to the spot where he had been sick. He put his hand down into the wet spew-soiled ivy. Stuck to its hilt in the roots was a thin-bladed knife.

He wrapped it in his handkerchief and put it carefully inside his shirt. He looked at his watch. Ten minutes had passed since he had begun his search. He walked through the house to the library. "Mrs. Lynes, Brod's had enough time to change. Will you show me where he is?"

Kenyon came toward him. "Of course, Officer. I took him to my room."

He followed her through the hall and up the stairs, aware of the unease he had left behind him in the library. At the top of the stairs Kenyon led him down the hall to a large room at a corner of the house. "I showed him Jack's closets and told him to choose whatever might suit him. But he's not here." She went to a door across the room and looked in, then shook her head. Angus looked about the room. He had a feeling that he had been there before, though he knew he had not. When he saw the chaise near the heavily draped window, he knew. It made his gut tighten. This was the setting where Bobby Horewood had been photographed.

"Brod's not here, Officer," Kenyon said. "I can't imagine what has happened to him."

Angus turned and ran out of the room, down the hall to the first floor. Outside in the driveway the sheriff sprawled, half standing, half lying, across the trunk of Angus's patrol car. He was moaning angrily to himself. He had his police revolver in his hand. The Chrysler convertible was missing from the drive.

"You stupid bastard," he said thickly as Angus came down the steps. "You let him get away again. I ought to shoot you instead of him."

CHAPTER 28

Angus let Rowe rage until he had no more words, then nursed him around the car and into the house. He stank of whiskey. Rowe demanded to know what had happened to his shotgun; when Angus told him he had put it away, the sheriff said, "Don't you forget I still got my revolver. That boy shows up, I'll get him."

Angus put the sheriff in a chair near the mantel. He wanted to take Rowe's gun, but he dared not antagonize the sheriff any more than necessary.

Kenyon Lynes had Maggie set out ice and decanters on a chest in a corner where Barrell, Glove, and Mathers all went as soon as they came in.

Lois Mathers greeted Mrs. Nailles coolly, and Nick Mathers, after a quick "I'm sorry," to her, took his drink and found a seat on the other side of the room from his wife. This and the sheriff's manner toward her upset Mrs. Nailles until Kenyon took her off to another room. They returned after five minutes, resumed their places. Mrs. Nailles did not recognize Rowe's or Mathers's presence. Selma Rillbon and Peaches appeared with Pat, Selma looking tense and disapproving. She had put on a hat and gloves and carried a pocketbook; it was appropriate, she seemed to be saying, when calling on a bereaved family. She murmured some consoling platitude to Kenyon and to Mrs. Nailles and took a seat to one side. Pat Rillbon stood behind her. Peaches dropped into a chair and sat looking about the room, clearly wishing that she was not there. She had changed into a dress.

Sally Carter Barrell went to fetch her husband and Maggie, after some protest, agreed to bring Serene to the library. The electricity was still off, and Maggie brought some candles with her which she put on a table. Pat Rillbon found some matches and lit four of them. Kenyon put them about the room; they helped to assist what little late afternoon light came through the windows.

Sally Carter Barrell resumed her place on the sofa; Kenyon was in her chair beside the fireplace and Biston Barrell pulled up a straight chair and was trying to appear removed and slightly amused at all the goings-on. Maggie and Serene had brought chairs from the hall and put them near the door. Cap Cumberley stood beside a window; Amy, warned by Sally Carter that her ex-husband was there, nodded and sat with her back to him.

They tried a little small talk but it died quickly and everyone looked to Angus. Cap Cumberley nodded at him with an indication of confidence and support. The sheriff said roughly, "All right, Bealle. Get on with it. And you better not fu-mess it up any more than you already have." He looked around for approval of his delicacy of language, but he got it only from Sally Carter's superior smile and a nod from her husband.

"I asked Mr. Cumberley to come here to see that things go right. I don't want to do anything that would mess this case up."

"Any more," Biston Barrell muttered.

"It ain't our mess," Maggie said loudly; Serene put a hand out to quiet her.

"Stop playing these games with us," Barrell said. "You know goddamn well it was Brod Nailles and you're trying to cover your hide because you let him get away."

"But Brod didn't—he couldn't have killed his father!" Mrs. Nailles cried out. "And Jack! Kenyon, you don't possibly believe—"

"I don't know what to believe," Kenyon said sharply. "Let's hear what this officer has to say."

"This is all your responsibility, Cumberley," Barrell said. "You're going to be held accountable for what goes on here today."

Cumberley did not answer him.

"Come on, Bitsy. Don't be so pompous." Fossy Glove tried to lighten the atmosphere without success.

"Mrs. Lynes, you understand, what I might say, it's not disrespect for Mr. Lynes, anything like that. It's part of my job."

"My husband was murdered, Mr. Bealle. If you know any-thing that will lead to who did it, you say what you have to."

Angus cleared his throat. "Yes, ma'am. I'm going to say what I know. Now, the two dead men were friends most of their lives. They went to college together and I guess there wasn't any way they couldn't know about each other, what the other one was like. I mean, for instance, there was that—that trouble at that fraternity party."

"Everybody knows about that," Amy Cumberley said impatiently. "That was years ago."

Selma Rillbon put her gloved hands to her mouth and sat rigidly while her husband put a hand on her shoulder.

"People's natures are hard to understand sometimes," Angus went on. "I mean, Mark Nailles had a nature that made him do some rotten things, that Mr. Lynes knew about, and some he probably didn't, but that didn't make too much difference, because they were still friends. Isn't that so, Mrs. Lynes?"

"Yes, I suppose it is. Jack tolerated a lot from Mark Nailles. More than I was willing to do."

"He knew about some of those things from when they were younger, but maybe not about some things that happened later. Like getting involved with young girls. There were probably other times, but I'm going to mention only one." He looked at the corner where Serene and her mother sat. Serene was looking straight at him, her mouth tense. "That was last Friday night before he was killed. Mr. Rillbon and Nailles had an argument about him showing attention to Peaches. That right, Mr. Rillbon?"

Pat's acknowledgment was little more than a cough. Peaches stirred and slouched lower in her chair when the eyes in the room turned toward her. Serene's face relaxed and she almost smiled at Angus.

"But what you don't know, Mr. Rillbon, is that Peaches and Nailles met again later. Isn't that so, Peaches?" The girl cut her eyes around at her father, saw the look on his face, and looked down at the floor. She did not answer Angus.

"I told him he was a fool to try anything," Amy said. "I knew that little tart would cause trouble."

"The first time, Brod Nailles was there," Angus said. "He

heard his father arguing with somebody, and he heard his father being threatened."

"I've already told you," Rillbon said. "It was me who had the argument, but that was all it was."

"First your wife and then your daughter," Biston Barrell said, his tone implying that one could expect nothing more. Pat moved forward quickly but stopped when Fossy Glove stood up and blocked his way.

Angus went on when Pat Rillbon had resumed his place. "But that argument happened between ten-thirty and eleven; Nailles wasn't killed until later. At the end of the fights."

"You know that for a fact?" Barrell asked.

"Several people saw him after that, including you, Mr. Barrell. Dr. Panthorpe says Nailles was killed by some sharp object. He found one of those steel spurs they use in cockfights in him."

"Cut him up pretty bad," the sheriff mumbled agreement. Nailles's widow turned her head to look away from him.

"The weapon that killed Mr. Lynes was a sharp blade. There's another kind of spur, called slashers."

"But they're not considered sporting to use around here," Barrell said. "Not even for murder."

"For God's sake, Bitsy!" Amy snapped. "Shut up!"

Angus was watching Kenyon Lynes as he talked to see if what he was saying would upset her, but she made no sign of emotion.

"What about those things you call slashers?" Fossy Glove asked.

"Mr. Rillbon kept them in a cupboard in the barn, along with the other gaffs."

"There you have it, then." Barrell's tone was final. "You're saying it was Rillbon?" Everyone but Barrell turned to look at the Rillbons. Selma Rillbon reached up and put her hand tightly on her husband's arm. Pat stared straight at Angus without blinking.

"He has the key to the cupboard, but he left it open for Bobby Horewood to use them at the fights." Angus looked about the room. "Do any of you know Bobby Horewood?" The question was put with as much ingenuousness as Angus's natural honesty could summon.

"Of course," Kenyon Lynes said quickly. "He's the young man at the Exxon station."

"Oh? Is that his name?" Barrell's question was meant to be as ingenuous as Angus's, but missed.

"I think I know the one you mean," Amy Cumberley said casually. "He was one of the handlers Friday night."

"He handled some of the birds for Mr. Lynes. He was in the shed at some time after Nailles and Rillbon argued."

"And he saw Nailles and Rillbon?" Barrell asked quickly.

"No. That was earlier. But Jack Lynes saw him there at the end of the fights. While Bobby was in the shed Mr. Lynes came looking for Nailles. He stood at the door and called and then went away."

"Unfortunately, Jack had had too much to drink that night," Barrell said. He took out a handkerchief and wiped his upper lip of the sweat that was beginning to show there. "Sorry, Kenyon, but you know it was so. It would be impossible now to prove what he might have seen, or said."

Kenyon did not acknowledge his comment.

"But what he saw must have killed him!" Lois Mathers spoke quickly. "If he went into the shed looking for Mark, he must have had some reason to think he was there. And if he saw something—saw who it was who had killed Mark—"

"Mr. Nailles wasn't dead when Mr. Lynes went in there. He must have been somewhere in the shed but he hadn't been killed."

"This what's his name—the young man—"

"Bobby Horewood, Mr. Barrell?"

"Yes. Is that what this Horewood told you?"

"He said that somebody came to the door, called for Nailles, then went away."

"Did he say it was Lynes?"

"No, Mr. Barrell. He said it was somebody who had had a lot to drink."

"What was Bobby doing there?" This from Nick Mathers.

"He was—" Angus stopped. Barrell's face was white and he looked as though he might be sick. "He told me he was there looking for something." He saw the look of relief flash across Barrell's face as the blood came back to his head.

"Looking for the gaffs he had lost?" Fossy Glove was guessing.

"He hadn't lost them then. He was there to meet somebody."

"I'm not surprised." Kenyon's voice was coolly acid. "He has a reputation around here, as I'm sure you know, Officer." She was speaking to Angus, but she looked in Amy's direction. Amy looked back at her calmly.

"Yes, ma'am."

"And you think he knows who it was who killed Mark?" Amy asked loudly. "If he didn't do it himself?"

"It's possible, yes, ma'am."

"Then why hasn't he told you? Sheriff—" she turned to face Rowe, and saw that the sheriff's head was down. He was asleep. "My God! What kind of police force have we got here? He's gone to sleep!" She got up, went across the room to the chair where the sheriff nodded. "You! Wake up!"

Rowe's head bobbed back and he looked quickly around the room. "Wha— Bealle, you get on with what you've got to say. We ain't got all day." He stared up at Amy, shifted in his chair, and cleared his throat. "You just sit down there, ma'am, and take it easy."

Amy stood her ground. "This is all nonsense. Two men have been murdered, and look what we've got. A drunken bum and a boy. Cap, can't you do something about this?"

Cumberley spoke for the first time. "Just sit down, Amy. Angus knows what he's doing." His voice was tired and lifeless. "You'll see."

"Then why hasn't he done something besides just stand here making a lot of speculations?"

"In good time, Amy. Just sit down, please."

She went back to her seat in silence.

"And you know who it is?"

"Yes, ma'am."

"And you're ready to prove it, here?"

"No, ma'am. Not until I can find Bobby Horewood."

"What the hell are you talking about, Bealle? You know damn well where to find Bobby Horewood." The sheriff was awake but not fully alert.

"No, sir. I went to his house, but he wasn't there."

"Well, you just go there and wait for him till he gets home."

"No, sir. Not until I'm through here."

"Do I understand that this Horewood person," Sally Carter spoke his name as though she were picking up something unclean. "This Bobby Horewood knows who committed these murders, and you stand there wasting time while he might be running off to God knows where?"

"He won't run off, Mrs. Barrell."

"This sounds like a lot of rash speculation, Officer." Barrell shifted in his chair. "You put a lot of faith in this young Horewood. How do you know you can trust him? He may be lying to save his own skin."

"You haven't said who he was meeting in that shed room?" Fossy Glove asked.

"No, sir, not yet."

Barrell turned to Cap Cumberley. "It seems to me, Cap, that you should stop this right now. This young man obviously is trying to intimidate all of us here; he hasn't any more idea of what happened to Mark and Jack than I do."

Cumberley shook his head. "He knows what he's doing, Bitsy."

"It's melodramatic nonsense," Sally Carter said. "Just like some silly television movie. I suppose you're going to say something idiotic, like 'The murderer is in this room.'"

"Yes, ma'am. I suppose I am."

Taken by surprise, Sally Carter sat up straight and there was a slight movement as each of the people in the room looked about at the others. As if to emphasize the melodrama, a lamp on a table beside the sofa flashed on and off and then came on as the electricity was restored. At the same time the doors to the library opened and Brod Nailles looked in. Bobby Horewood, peering anxiously at the assembled room, stood beside him.

CHAPTER 29

The sudden return of the electric lights and the appearance of Bobby Horewood sent a charge of energy through the library. Biston Barrell half rose from his chair in a spontaneous muscle reaction; Amy and Kenyon looked quickly at each other and then back to the door; Peaches sat up and smiled knowingly; and Pat Rillbon moved from one side of his wife's chair to the other as though to come between her and the man at the door. Mrs. Nailles's attention was on Brod. Serene and Maggie, whose chairs were on the same wall with the doors, had to lean forward to see who was there. Cap Cumberley, leaning against a windowsill, stood up straight, recrossed his arms, and leaned back the way he had been.

Bobby Horewood acknowledged Amy and Kenyon with equal nods and tentative smiles. This over, he stared straight at Sally Carter until she dropped her eyes; looked insolently at Biston, who stared idly at the ceiling; then turned his head and recognized Serene with a nod while he ran his tongue lightly over his white teeth. There was no doubting the message he flashed to each of them. He passed over the Gloves and the Mathers with a quick glance, holding his attention on the women for an extra second each. For Selma Rillbon he had a small sideways nod which made her look at her lap. Finally his eyes met Peaches's and held them while the room waited for Angus. Peaches squirmed deliciously in her chair as she watched him from under her long lashes.

Sheriff Rowe pulled himself painfully up out of the wing chair and tried to reach for his revolver but found a cushion in his way. Before he could get his weapon out Angus saw what he was up to and moved across the room to stop him.

Rowe growled something under his breath when Angus put his hand on his arm and held it there. His movement broke the surprise of Bobby's entrance, but nobody fell back into the private concerns that had filled the room before he came in. He had shifted the sands on which they stood. Brod moved across the room to stand behind his mother.

"Well, we're all here," Amy Cumberley said with false brightness. "Now we can get on with it. Point your finger, young man." Bobby still stood inside the doorway. He looked down at his hands, made his thumbs and fingers into mock pistols, and without changing his expression fired invisible bullets at Amy. She looked away, her face flushing quickly.

"You should be cautioned, Horewood," Barrell tried to sound commanding, but there was a pleading tone to his voice. "You should be careful what you say; don't make accusations you can't back up. The consequences can be serious."

"Oh, stop it, Bitsy," Amy's brightness was replaced by irritation. "You're not the investigating officer here. For all we know, you might be the principal suspect."

"Now, just a moment, Amy—"

"Please!" Mrs. Nailles raised her voice. "Let the officer here get this over with."

"He was just where you said he'd be," Brod said. "That was a neat move, making them think I'd run off!"

"He said you needed some help," Bobby said. "So's I'm not in any trouble."

Angus shook his head. "What I need is for you to say just what it was went on in the shed Friday night."

"Hey, look now, man. I told you I don't know anything about that murder. He was alive when I left there."

"You said you were in the shed with—" Angus turned, indicated Barrell with his head. "—with Mr. Barrell here." Barrell's mouth was open; he was having difficulty breathing.

"Sure. That's right. We were there, like you say. This fellow comes to the door and calls for this other guy. Nailles. It was like he was drunk or something."

"Did he see you?"

"Must have, but he cut out right away."

"Did you see who it was?"

"It was Lynes."

"What did you do?"

"I—we were—through—so I cut out. This other guy was standing inside the shed, beside the door. It was dark, but not that dark."

"Did Barrell go with you?"

"No. He stayed there."

"Yes, but I—" Barrell had trouble finding his voice. He stood up. "For God's sake, Cap, you can't let him make them think I killed Mark!"

"Go on, Angus," Cumberley said quietly.

Barrell turned to the room and saw that there was no refuge there. His last appeal was to his wife. "My God! You can't think that I—"

"Biston. Please, sit down and be quiet."

Barrell sat on the edge of his chair; he looked as though he was going to cry. "All right," Barrell said, trying to control his voice. "Mark was there. He must have been there when we—Horewood and I came in. We'd been talking earlier about the—co—" he cleared his throat as though choking on the word. "—birds he had been handling and we—he was going to—I wanted to—to hear more about them. When he left, Mark came —came to where I was and—" Barrell took a deep breath. "He'd been goddamned offensive to Sally Carter earlier. I wasn't going to stand for that, so I left. That was the last time I saw him."

"Why didn't you tell me that before, Mr. Barrell?"

"Well I—I didn't think it made that much difference."

"My God!" Amy said loudly.

Angus turned to Bobby. "When you left the shed, did you have the gaffs with you?"

"I told you, man, I put them in my car."

"But one of them was found in Nailles's body," Barrell said quickly.

"Hey! Wait a minute—" Bobby's voice was angry. "I put them in the map compartment. When I got back to my car. You saw I had one of them at the garage, Angus. The other could have fell off when we was in the barn. It would have been easy, considering what—"

"Wait a minute." Fossy Glove held up his hands. "You say that Cumberley was there at the cockfights?"

"That's right."

"And he saw Barrell in Horewood's car with him?"

"You're trying to frame me, damn you, Glove!" Barrell jumped up and waved a hand at Glove. "Horewood offered me a drink, and that's all we were doing. Tell him, Horewood."

"Sure. That's what we were doing."

Barrell whirled around to face his wife. "They're trying to say I killed Mark! Sally Carter, I—"

Barrell's wife came across to him and put a hand on his arm. "Just sit down, Biston. Let these men finish. Nobody's said you killed anybody." She waited until he was sitting, then returned to her own place. "If you know who killed my brother, Officer, please say so. Now."

Angus did not answer her. He turned to face Maggie Allan. "Saturday morning, Mrs. Allan, Mrs. Lynes asked you to wash some clothes that had bloodstains on them."

Maggie nodded. "They was a mess. I couldn't do nothing with them, so I told her Mrs. Cumberley would have to throw them out."

"What did you do with them?"

"I still got them."

"Everybody knows how the stains got there," Amy said. "It was chicken blood. Bitsy was there, he got the same thing."

"Bitsy's clothes were ruined," his wife said. "I will have to throw his trousers away."

"I'll have to take them, Mrs. Barrell. And yours, too, Mrs. Cumberley."

"This is outrageous!" Barrell protested.

"You should have said something earlier, Officer. Yesterday, when I gave them to Kenyon, you were in the hall." Amy said. "Maggie just said she has already tried to wash them."

"Yes, ma'am. That was my mistake."

Sheriff Rowe spoke from his chair. "This ain't getting us anywhere. Why ain't you going after the boy?"

"Because he didn't kill them."

"Jack Lynes must have thought so," Barrell jumped in. "Nick Mathers told you he kept saying Saturday night something about putting it on the boy."

"Doing it to the boy, Bitsy." Mathers corrected him.

"Whatever, Nick. Who else could he have meant?"

Angus turned to Peaches. "You told me you came back to the barn after your father sent you home. Did you see anybody around the shed?"

Peaches's attention had been riveted on Bobby, and Angus had to repeat the question before she understood. She looked at him and then at her father, shook her head without speaking. Pat Rillbon's face was dark with fury.

Peaches worked at the edge of a fingernail with intense concentration before she cast her head up. "Her." She threw a hand in Amy Cumberley's direction.

"I've already told you I went looking for Mark when he didn't come back. But that was after the fights. I saw her there. I didn't think she had seen me, but apparently she did."

"Did you find Mr. Nailles?"

"No. To be honest, he had been—unpleasant earlier, and I was angry with him."

"So you went back to the house. Did you see anybody else?"

Amy hesitated. "There was somebody in a car parked near the shed. It was dark; I didn't pay much attention. Most of the rest of the cars were gone."

"It was Mr. Cumberley." Angus said it quietly. Amy looked around at her ex-husband and then back at Angus. Cumberley shifted his stance, becoming more alert than he had appeared. "Mr. Cumberley told me he saw you." He kept his eyes on Cumberley, but he was not prepared for what Cumberley did. From his place by the window he moved forward quickly, seizing Amy by an arm and pulling her from her seat. "Amy! Don't you know? Don't you realize? It was somebody like Nailles who killed Emily! Our daughter would be alive today, if it weren't for men like him!" She tried to pull away from him, but Cumberley held her fast. "Don't you care about that?"

"Let go of me, Cap. You're hurting my arm!"

"NO! You've got to listen. We ruined our lives, and we let Emily ruin hers. Do you know what some man did to her? Do you know? What kind of woman are you that you can let a man like that touch you?"

Amy tried to pull his hand away, turning to Angus for help. "Officer, make this man let go of me!"

The sheriff had risen clumsily from his chair but Angus was across the room before he could move. "Mr. Cumberley. Let her go. Now." Cumberley stared at him, then almost as though he were discarding her, let Amy's arm go. Amy stepped back to the mantel and stood rubbing her upper arm. Cumberley looked around the room, his eyes going from one face to another. They were all watching him. He turned away and went to the chest in a corner near where Serene and her mother sat, poured a drink from a decanter, and put it down in a gulp. It was plain this was not the first drink he had had that day.

"Don't do this to yourself, Cap!" Despite her anger, Amy's voice was concerned. "You mustn't start that again. You've been doing so well!"

"Doing well? For God's sake! I've been going through hell. While you've been shacking up with that—that perverted molester of children—for Christ's sake, Amy! Don't you KNOW?" He turned to Angus. "I told you I was there Friday night, and I told you I saw Horewood and somebody else in his car. I didn't know it was you, Barrell, until I saw you get out and go back to the barn. And I don't give a damn what you were doing there, although I can hazard a good guess."

"Now look here, Cumberley—"

Cumberley took a deep breath. "I saw Horewood and Barrell in Horewood's car. They were doing just what Bitsy said—having a drink from a bottle."

"That's disgusting, Biston," his wife said icily.

"I'll tell you what's disgusting," Cumberley said. "After they had gone, I went there and found the bottle in the glove compartment. I'd already had more than enough to drink. I'd started drinking when I got home Friday night. But I took the bottle and I drank what was left."

"Hey, man," Horewood spoke up. "It was almost a full bottle."

Cumberley went across the room and stood before the Rillbons. "You listen to me, both of you. Get her away from here. Get her away before the same things happen to her. It's not too late, Selma!"

Angus held up his hands. "Mr. Cumberley. Don't say any more."

Cumberley opened his mouth to say something, closed it, and dropped his hands in a gesture of futility. "You told me earlier that you thought Pat Rillbon killed those two men. You said—"

Selma Rillbon stood up from her chair and her high-pitched sound split through the room. "NO! It's not so! He didn't do it!"

Her husband reached out to pull her back, but she shook free of him and seized Angus's arms. "You can't say that. They deserved what they got!"

Angus pushed her back. "Mrs. Rillbon. Before you say anything more, you ought to—"

"It's my fault. Punish me! Not him!"

"—you ought to hear what I've got to say."

"Please! I told you. I've sinned against God, and I'm forever damned. The Lord said thou shalt not kill, thou shalt not commit adultery—"

"Please, Selma!" Pat Rillbon put an arm around her shoulder.

"But I have to be punished. I've sinned. With him!" She pointed a finger at Bobby Horewood, who had been watching alertly. He looked at Angus and made an almost imperceptible shrug of his shoulders, telegraphing a silent, "You see, I told you so."

"My God, I don't believe this!" Amy said, half laughing.

"He came here when Pat was away, seeing about those chickens. I told him he was wicked and sinful, and he—there was something—" She put her head down suddenly, her hands across her mouth, and sank to the floor. Pat Rillbon stooped down and lifted her gently up and led her back to her chair. Cumberley went to the chest to pour himself another drink. Bobby Horewood rose on his toes, alert for possible trouble. His eyes moved about quickly, meeting the stare of each person in the room.

"Really, Sheriff," Fossy Glove had been sitting silently watching the exchange. "Don't you think there's been enough of this? If this young man has any accusations to make, let's hear them."

"Yes, I absolutely agree," Barrell said.

Rowe cleared his throat and muttered. "All right, Bealle. You going to charge somebody, you do it now. Understand?"

"Yes, sir." He had to breathe deeply to keep his voice from

breaking. He reached into his shirt pocket, drawing out a folded set of papers, then reached inside his shirt and took out the handkerchief with the knife. "Mr. Cumberley, you said I had to do whatever I thought was right. I'm sorry, sir."

CHAPTER 30

Cumberley dropped his tumbler when he saw the papers in Angus's hand. He turned, the decanter in his hand, to look at Amy.

Bobby Horewood saw the handle of the knife under the handkerchief and whirled toward the door.

Sheriff Rowe shoved himself out of his chair shouting, "Stop him, Bealle!" as Horewood pushed past Cumberley. Cumberley reached out to stop him, swinging the decanter in a wide arc. Bobby fell back against the door as the bottle shattered against his head. Blood ran down his face to his bare chest, but he did not fall. He grabbed at Cumberley as the older man pushed past him, trying to get to Amy.

Angus had Cumberley by the arm when the sheriff fired. Angus felt his arm go limp, but there was no immediate pain as the bullet cut through his bicep and struck Cumberley under his shoulder from the back. In the confusion of screams and shouts, Cumberley opened the door and fell into the hall. As the pain ran down his arm and up again, Angus saw Cumberley rise to his feet and then fall against the round table in the hall.

He lay there, face down. There was little blood showing on his back where the sheriff's bullet had entered, but blood from his punctured lung ran from his open mouth. He was conscious but he did not struggle when Fossy Glove and Nick Mathers lifted him and stretched him out on the floor in the hall. Lois Mathers put a coat under his head while Tottsy Glove tried to calm Amy.

The sheriff tried to take charge, but Angus told him angrily to stay out of the way. He stood half-stunned in the background while Angus and the other men tried to look after the two wounded men.

It was thirty minutes before the rescue squad arrived, another fifteen before they drove off to the University Hospital in

Charlottesville. Angus let Billy Hogshead bind his arm, then got into the ambulance with Cumberley and Bobby Horewood. Pat Rillbon followed with the sheriff in his patrol car. Angus sat beside Cumberley and listened while Cumberley talked in rasping whispers until the squad attendant made him stop.

By the time they reached the hospital Cumberley was unconscious. Bobby said his head hurt but insisted he did not want any further treatment. Angus left him arguing with the admitting nurse.

The sheriff, defending his actions in what had happened, declared it was his duty to stay with Cumberley, who had been wheeled away to an operating room. Pat drove Angus back to Copperfields after his wound had been treated. His arm ached and it was cumbersome with the bandage, but he had to see the matter ended. He sent Pat to fetch Peaches and Mrs. Rillbon.

Fossy Glove and Nick Mathers met Angus in the drive and followed him inside. Maggie answered the door and nodded toward the library, where he found Brod and his mother, Mrs. Glove and Amy Cumberley. Kenyon Lynes, Mrs. Nailles said, had gone to her room and had taken something to calm herself. Lois Mathers was with her. The Barrells came down from their room when Brod went to tell them that Angus had returned. Mrs. Barrell sat tight-lipped on the sofa as her husband poured himself a drink and found a seat opposite her. Maggie and Serene came in and took their seats, their manner saying clearly that they intended to see the spectacle through to the end.

The pain in his arm Angus could endure if he did not move it, but the pain he felt inside was something else.

Before the room had settled, Lois Mathers came in and found a seat near Amy Cumberley. There were dark circles under her eyes, her body sagged in a way that made her look old. Mrs. Barrell seemed untouched by what had happened; she maintained an air of distant interest. Now that the threat of exposure had been lifted, Biston Barrell assumed an air of detached amusement. Mrs. Nailles, showing the strains of the day, sat calmly with her son. The Mathers and the Gloves were subdued. Angus told them that Cumberley's condition was critical.

"I simply cannot believe this of Cap," Tottsy Glove said for perhaps the fourteenth time. "He's the last person—"

"He had been drinking; you could see that," Fossy said. "I thought he had given all that up. Too bad."

"But what made him do it, for God's sake? I can understand his being upset about his daughter's death; all that business to the Rillbons about getting their daughter out before it was too late." Tottsy Glove went on. "What would make him so concerned about her now that he would want to kill Mark? And Jack? Why Jack?"

"We'll just have to wait to see what the police learn from him when he recovers." Nick Mathers poured himself a drink.

"If he recovers," Fossy said.

"Well, at least we can put it all behind us now."

"Put it behind?" Amy Cumberley looked up. "Is this all that Cap means to you? We can't just put it behind us. We'll never be the same, any of us."

"It's hard on you, Amy, I'm sure," Sally Carter said. "Cap was your husband once, but Mark was my brother. He was killed in cold blood—"

"Amy's right," Lois Mathers said. "Nothing can be the same from now on."

Fossy Glove spoke up. "Bealle here has cleared it up quickly, thank God; now if we can just keep it out of the papers as much as possible—"

"That's all that matters? Keeping it out of the papers?" Amy was angry. "How in God's name are you going to keep this out of the papers. When the trial comes up—"

"If we're lucky, perhaps there won't be a trial," Barrell said quietly. "It's quite possible that Cumberley won't survive that gunshot wound. If he doesn't, there won't be any trial."

"You'd like that, wouldn't you, Bitsy?" Amy looked about the room. "Cap was right about you, all of you. All of us. Oh God, what a mess." She put her head in her hands, sobbing. Lois Mathers put an arm around her shoulder.

"But how did you find out that Cumberley killed them?" Mathers stirred the ice in his drink with a forefinger.

"I never said he did," Angus said. "I said I was sorry I had to do this to him."

"If you mean he didn't murder them," Fossy Glove said. "Then who did? Did he see who did it?"

Angus waited for a long moment before he answered. "He had been drinking heavily all afternoon. But he remembers what happened Friday night."

"Please, can't we start at the beginning?" Tottsy Glove spoke impatiently. "I don't understand any of this."

"Mrs. Cumberley, what I say is—will be hard for you."

"Never mind that. If it's my fault, I've got to know."

"No, ma'am. I'm not talking about fault. I grew up here in Bushanna County, and I don't know a lot about how people—people like you live. You're supposed to be people that other folks look up to. But what you do to each other, well, I just don't understand."

"Please," Sally Carter Barrell said. "Spare us the moralizing and just tell us what happened to my brother."

"Yes, ma'am. Mrs. Cumberley, when your daughter died last year, it was because she was pregnant, and she had an abortion."

"Yes. I know that."

"Did you know that she and Brod knew each other?"

"They've known each other all their lives. But Emily wasn't interested in Brod. She said he was being a nuisance. I'm sorry, Brod." He brushed her apology aside. "You can't think Brod was the father."

"No, but Brod found out who was. It was his father."

"Oh my God!" Amy cried out. Lois Mathers took her hand, but Amy pulled quickly away.

"He followed them the night she died. It was after that he and his father had the fight. Then Brod left school and about six months ago he turned up at the commune at Sweet Valley." While Angus talked, Brod sat staring straight ahead of him. "At the commune he met a woman who is studying medicine at the University. He told her about Emily and his father. Last week she showed him something from a medical journal that made him believe that his father had been directly responsible for Emily Cumberley's death. Not that he was. She was just making mischief." Brod looked up sharply, started to say something, then stopped.

Angus went on. "She sent a copy of the article to Mr. Cumberley. He had it in his office Friday afternoon when I was there;

I didn't know then what it was, but I saw it on his desk. Annabel showed it to me Saturday night and told me she had sent it to people she thought ought to have it, but I didn't connect it with Mr. Cumberley. Yesterday afternoon I talked to Mr. Cumberley in his office, and while we were talking he balled something up and threw it away. I went to his office this afternoon and found it there." He reached in his shirt pocket and pulled out the tightly folded sheets.

"What's it about?"

"Sorry, Mr. Glove. I'm not going to say." He put the papers back in his pocket. "It upset him enough to start him to drinking again, and he drove out here Friday night. He told me he wanted to see what was going on at the cockfight because he was concerned about the sheriff being there, and whether there were any laws being broken. That's what he wanted to think, but he told me in the ambulance he was also looking for Mark Nailles.

"He got there about ten-thirty, or a few minutes earlier. Mr. Rillbon saw him. Brod got there a few minutes later. He saw his father and Peaches together, and he heard Mr. Rillbon arguing with Nailles. That was about ten minutes or so after Mr. Cumberley got there. It was maybe twenty minutes later when Mr. Cumberley saw Bobby Horewood and Mr. Barrell sitting in Bobby's car drinking; when they left, he went to the car and got the bottle of whiskey.

"He sat in his car near the shed and drank most of the bottle. He saw Peaches come to a corner of the shed, then Mark Nailles came around and the two of them went around the shed. That must have been around eleven-thirty. He sat there and got more and more angry at Nailles and what he was doing."

"We weren't doing anything!" Peaches said petulantly. "We were just talking, that's all."

Pat Rillbon put a rough hand on her shoulder. "Be quiet, you!" His wife sat staring hard at the carpet in front of her.

"When he got out of his car to follow them he hit the bottle against the door and it broke and cut his hand. The sheriff and I found the broken bottle, and we saw the drops of blood leading around the shed. When he got to the back of the barn, he saw Nailles and Peaches."

"I told you we were just talking!"

Selma Rillbon stood up quickly, slapped her daughter hard across the face, and sat down again without looking at her. Pat reached out and touched her head, gently. Peaches ran out of the room, crying and slamming the door hard behind her. Fossy Glove rose as if to fetch her back, but Angus stopped him. "It's okay, Mr. Glove. Let her go."

Angus continued. "He turned around and went back to his car. He saw Peaches go off and Nailles come around to the door of the shed. Nailles heard somebody coming and ducked inside as Barrell then Bobby Horewood came along and went in. A few minutes later Jack Lynes came from the barn and stood in the doorway calling for Mark Nailles, then left. Right after that Bobby Horewood came out and went to the barn, and a few minutes later Barrell came out, went to Bobby's car and then ran back to the shed, stepped in the door, then walked off around the barn. Mr. Cumberley sat there trying to get his head clear enough to drive off. He doesn't remember much about driving home except that he passed Lynes walking as he drove out the lane. He was in bad shape when I talked to him Saturday afternoon, but he wasn't drunk. He was depressed, and hung over. He told me about his daughter's death, and that's when he threw the sheets of paper into the fireplace."

"And you think Jack was killed because he saw who had killed Mark?" Lois Mathers asked, her voice a whisper.

"Jack had had a lot to drink," her husband said. "I should have made him go to bed. I suppose it's my fault; he said he was going to watch television."

"It's nobody's fault, Nick," Charlotte Glove said. "How could you have known?"

"Nevertheless, I feel badly about it."

Angus felt the pain returning to his arm as the injection he had been given wore off. He was suddenly so tired he wondered if he could remain standing. He knew that if he did not get outside where he could breathe fresh cool air, he was going to throw up.

"Lynes was killed because he saw what was going on inside the shed." Angus took a deep breath. "We'll have a trial, Mr. Barrell. Bobby Horewood said he lost his knife. I know how he could have dropped it in the shed, and how the murderer could easily come on it, even in the dark. I found it tonight, stuck in the ivy below the terrace, where the murderer threw it after he killed Lynes. All you have to do is answer one question, Mr. Barrell. Why did you telephone the sheriff to tell him Brod was coming here?"

"Becau—" Barrell's voice was a squeak. "Because I thought you—thought you were looking for him. You—" He had sat up in his chair, looking anxiously around the room.

"No. You wanted to keep us thinking it was Brod who did it. Mr. Barrell, I have to warn you, you have the right to remain sil—"

CHAPTER 31

Before Angus could finish, Barrell gave a high-pitched scream, turned, and ran toward the door. Pat Rillbon put his foot out and sent him sprawling. He lay there sobbing until Angus pulled him to his feet. There was a wide spot on the carpet where Barrell had wet his trousers. Mrs. Barrell said something incoherent and slid to the floor in a faint.

While Lois Mathers and Charlotte Glove tried to revive Mrs. Barrell, Angus handcuffed her husband and stood him against the door frame to keep him from falling to the floor. Sally Carter, supported by the two women, stumbled from the room without looking at her husband.

Fossy Glove stood looking from Barrell to the wet spot on the floor and back, his face changing from distaste to disbelief. "Jesus Christ! Barrell? Why, in the name of God?"

Angus drew a deep breath, looked at the women remaining in the room, and told them what Bobby said they were doing when Jack Lynes came in the shed.

Nick Mathers said, "Well I'll be damned! That's what he meant about 'doing it to the boy?' Did you know that about Barrell, Fossy?"

"There was some talk when we were in school, but Jesus! And Mark was in there, watching the whole thing. But how did he get hold of the knife?"

"It must have fallen off Bobby's belt and Barrell found it when he crawled behind the tractor." Angus looked at Barrell, who nodded his head rapidly up and down. "Nailles saw what it was they were doing. After Bobby left, he confronted Barrell, and I'd guess he was rough on him." Angus kept his eyes on Barrell, who stared back at him as if mesmerized, his head nodding. "Barrell lost his temper and attacked Nailles, stabbed him with the knife, then went to Bobby's car to put it away."

"But what about the gaff?" Mathers asked. "How did it get there?"

"Barrell found them in Horewood's car." Fossy Glove was guessing, but Barrell continued to nod hypnotically. "Instead of putting the knife there, he kept it, took one of the gaffs and planted it in Nailles. Right?" As his two friends stared at him, Barrell nodded rapidly, his legs gave way and he sank to the floor.

"And then he killed Jack because Jack had seen him with the boy, and guessed that Nailles must have caught them, too." Mathers put a hand to his head, looked as though he was going to be sick, and walked out of the room.

"So that was what Jack and Bitsy were quarreling about yesterday during the game." Fossy Glove shook his head as if to deny what he now understood.

"And he had that knife with him all day, planning to kill Jack." Amy Cumberley, who had been sitting silently on the sofa, stood up, her eyes tearful. Glove put an arm around her shoulder and led her into the hall.

Angus turned to Serene, who had been sitting with her mother watching the scene. "You said this looked like a woman's crime. You shouldn't be so hard on women."

Serene shook her head. "That's not fair to women, and you know it."

"I'm sorry. You're right. But thank you, anyway. It helped me understand some of this."

Serene stood and leaned forward, put her arms around his shoulders and kissed him gently. "Thanks for your help, too, Angus."

He walked out of the house with Barrell, put his prisoner inside his patrol car, and leaned against it while he took deep breaths of air. He was glad to be out of the house; he would leave the people inside to their own problems. He felt sorry for Mrs. Barrell, but not that sorry.

There was no jail in Bushanna County, so he drove Barrell to the lockup in Charlottesville.

He found Sheriff Rowe at the hospital, waiting to hear from the doctors on Cumberley's condition. On the promise that he would be called as soon as anything was known, Angus persuaded the sheriff to go home with him. By the time he reached his parents' house, it was almost morning. He found his way to his room and fell into bed.

It was four hours later when his mother waked him to tell him he had a telephone call. A doctor at the hospital told him that Cumberley had survived the operation and was likely to recover. Angus asked about Bobby Horewood and was told that he had disappeared from the emergency room before he had been treated. His mother did not question him when he went back to his room without telling her what had happened.

Angus lay on his bed and looked out the window at the morning light in the woods behind the house. He thought about the events that had brought him to this morning. If Peaches hadn't behaved the way she did, would Nailles have followed her outside? If Annabel hadn't meddled with the information she had found, would Mr. Cumberley have started drinking and gone to Copperfields? If he had not remembered that day at Solverson's pool, would he have asked Bobby about Barrell? If it hadn't been for Bobby, would any of this have happened? If . . . if . . . if . . .

He didn't know if he had dreamed it, but sometime in the ending night he thought he had heard a sound, half sigh, half groan. He didn't know what it meant, but he knew that something he had known was gone for good and that life would not ever be the same as it had been.

About the Author

William Maner was born in South Carolina and grew up in Virginia where he and his family make their home. He served as an officer aboard destroyer escorts in the Atlantic and Mediterranean during World War II and later taught English at the University of Richmond. Mr. Maner is the author of numerous short stories as well as two other books for the Crime Club, *Die of a Rose,* and *The Image Killer.*